The Other Side

A Haunting Dystopian Tale

Book 3

∞

Heather Carson

Table of Contents

Chapter 1

∞

Dark clouds rolled in quickly across the sky, mercifully saving me from the afternoon of forced smiles and handshakes. I'd been feeling like a clueless puppet as I was paraded around to meet the various representatives in attendance. *There is no way I'm remembering any of these names.* I'd glared at Alister more times than I could count, but he seemed to be enjoying himself and didn't notice.

As the fat raindrops began to splatter against the hot sidewalks, we raced to the waiting vehicles. I was emotionally drained and slumped gratefully onto the back seat of the sedan. The downpour rolled in rivulets against the glass of the car window. Alister was drenched as he climbed in after me.

"Serves you right!" I yelled after he closed the door behind him. "What the hell did you just do to me?"

"Are you mad?" The corner of his mouth raised seductively, and I pressed my back against the opposite door.

"Of course I'm mad. What do I know about being a politician? And you didn't even warn me! The whole ride over here you could have said something. Anything!" My whole body was shaking. I couldn't tell if it was from the chill of being wet or the total outrage at the situation.

"You were so cute though, little deer. Sacrificing yourself in marriage to me. I wanted to hear you talk," Alister laughed.

My cheeks flushed. "So, you let me ramble on like an idiot instead of telling me you were about to sacrifice me to the wolves instead."

The humor fell from his face and he stared at me intently. "You won't be sacrificed anywhere. I would never have forced you into a marriage you didn't want. We aren't even allowed to get married unless I revoke your title. No harm will come to you as my running mate. Being labeled in this position affords you a certain measure of protection. Your name will give you power and safety."

"Where was Robert's protection?" I crossed my arms as the vehicle's engine roared to life. Alister looked down to the floorboard.

"That was different. I am nothing like my aunt. Roger was like a father to me." The pain in his voice caused my heart to break. I scooted closer to him.

"I know," I whispered softly. "Well, what am I supposed to do now?"

His eyes lit up as he leaned back next to me, smiling that oh so enchanting grin. "What do you want to do, little deer? The world is ours."

*

"There is something we need to discuss." Professor Berlin drained his coffee mug and set it back down on the dining room table. Two of the men dressed in blue, that were stationed outside the front door since the nomination ceremony, quickly filled their cups and exited the room. I watched them uncomfortably. Alister promised it was only routine for government officials to have guards, but it was hard to get used to their silent presence.

"I'm listening," I said as soon as we were alone.

"As much as I understand President Macavay's rationale for electing you as his second, I have doubts that you are prepared to handle this role." The professor smiled at me fondly.

"You and me both," I grumbled as I put my chin in my hands. "What am I supposed to do about it? He's already made his decision, without consulting me I might add."

"I'm not sure you would have liked the other option either," he chuckled, "but President Macavay is young and he believes nothing can harm him. If something were to happen to him, then it would fall on your shoulders to lead the country." The weight of his words sank heavily like a stone in my stomach.

"I don't think I can do that," I said. "I wouldn't even know where to start."

"Exactly." He pointed his finger at me. "You need at least some minimal training in this field. President Macavay doesn't want to overwhelm you right now, but I feel you are smart enough to handle this. Am I correct?"

"Yes," I nodded weakly. "I can try."

"Perfect." The professor stood and gathered his books from the table. "I'll see you in my office this afternoon."

*

The leaves on the trees in the courtyard were beginning to wither and the tips were turning yellow. I watched them dance in the late summer breeze through the open kitchen window.

"If you are not going to help, go sit in the chair." Freida nudged me with her hip.

"I'm helping." I turned the apple over in my hand and resumed peeling its skin. Steam rose from the large pot on the stove that held the canning jars. I placed the naked apple in the basket next to Freida.

"You shouldn't be in here anyway," she sighed. "Not with your fancy new job title and all."

"Please." I rolled my eyes and laughed. "You know I want to be in here. I need the distraction now more than ever."

"What's on your mind, child?" She sliced deftly through another apple leaving only the slightest sliver of a core.

Fear. Doubt. Confusion… The words played tug of war in my mind. I shook my head.

"Just trying to process everything. Less than a year ago I was living in my abandoned city apartment in downtown LA with my friends while working as a slave in the realm. Now I'm standing here in another city clear across the country with one friend who is a spirit and the other is married into the mafia family. Plus, you know, that fancy new job title. It's a lot to take in," I shrugged.

"That's what happens when you are young." Freida held the knife suspended in midair as she turned to me. "You crash around on the waves of life until you find your place in the world. If you're lucky, things slow down once you get there."

"I hope I'm lucky." I smiled at her. "How is your son doing at the university?"

"Oh, my Odan…" Her eyes, that were buried deep in her ruddy cheeks, sparkled brightly as she spoke about her son. I let her excited voice soothe me into a peaceful lull as I worked my way through peeling the bucket of apples.

Chapter 2

∞

"What have you seen so far in your travels of the world?" Professor Berlin looked up from his yellow papered notebook as I took a seat in the chair in front of his desk.

"An empty desert, crumbling buildings, and people living hard lives," I shrugged. "There's not much left to see."

"Look deeper," the professor said. "Start with your encounters with the people."

I remembered the village at the base of the Ruby Mountains and pictured Brayson working in the fields with Fallon's team. *That wasn't right. Vorie said he was building a barn now.* My thoughts drifted to the life on Freida's street and the bustle of the town market where Genie lived. *I need to write her a letter...*

"The people are all working. They are doing what it takes to survive. There aren't many that I know out west, but there seem to be more of them here."

"And why do they work?" he asked. "Why do they stay in this world instead of going to the realm?"

"That I don't really know. I'd like to think it's because they want to live despite how hard it is."

"Bingo." The professor smiled. "It's the stubborn primitive urge to have a body and use it."

"I'm not sure that's a bad thing," I sighed as I waited for another of his eternal spiritual lectures.

"Nevertheless," he continued, shocking me. "It is a hardened existence. The government makes life easier by maintaining the law and aiding those who need it. People give up a certain amount, whether through labor or a percentage of goods, in order to receive government services."

My forehead creased as I thought about this. "That really doesn't make the government any different than the mafia. The mafia gives us stuff in exchange for our work."

"It's much different." He placed the notebook on his desk. "The mafia doesn't give people a choice whereas the government encourages voting and active participation."

"And does the government allow the people the choice to not abide by its laws?" I bit my lip as I processed his words.

"What a curious question." He stared at me lost in thought for a moment. "One we will come back to another day. Today, let's explain how parliament works…"

I tried hard to focus as he explained the process of government, but my mind kept traveling back to the faces of the people I'd met.

"What if we focus on making the world less harsh? What if we make it a place where people actually want to live?" I suddenly interrupted him.

"Still clinging to hope for this life I see." He rubbed a hand over his tired eyes. "But you are missing the point. This life is only temporary. The realm is eternal. It's a waste of effort to focus on giving people a nice existence here when it will all eventually fade away."

"No disrespect." I leaned forward in my chair. "But I think you are wrong. I see people who still want to be here, and I've seen their struggles. Focusing on this life, no matter how temporary it is, is not a waste of effort. What's the purpose of having a life at all if we don't really live it?"

"You never cease to surprise me with your questions," Professor Berlin smiled. "But the realm is so much more powerful than this meager existence."

"The realm will always be there," I groaned. "Why is it so important that we focus on it right now?"

"There is more to this than you are ready to understand." His eyes shifted slightly, and I got the faintest hint that he deliberately was keeping something from me. He fumbled for his notebook and pen. "Where were we now?"

I watched his face as he read through the texts and recited notes he'd written about basic government procedure. The shift in the conversation was soon forgotten. I became too wrapped up in formulating my own plan to save the world.

*

Marley Macavay's trial was scheduled for the following day. Freida told me they had somehow convinced Roger Cannon to visit from the realm and testify. I'm not going to lie; I was beyond excited to attend. I wanted to watch her get indicted after what she put me through and part of me hoped I'd get the chance to give Roger a piece of my mind. *He could have warned me who I was dealing with instead of just giving me a random name...*

When Alister arrived to pick me up, his eyes were downcast and distant.

"What's wrong?" I asked as I climbed into the back of the car.

"Marley hung herself last night," he sighed. "The trial is canceled."

"She got away scot-free?" My eyes opened wide. "That really sucks." The car began to move down the street. "Where are we going then?"

"We've been summoned to the private government board meeting," he explained.

"Oh, like an executive session," I nodded.

"Where did you hear that term?" His lips curled into a playful smile.

"I've been studying." I raised my chin and watched the landscape roll past the window.

"I'd like to study with you," Alister whispered seductively as he moved closer to me.

"Maybe later." I put my hand firmly on his chest. "I want to look professional for the board and you'll rumple my outfit."

*

A dusty old room with a conference table in the center held a group of dusty old men planted firmly in their chairs. Their sharp eyes sized me up distrustfully as I entered. I would have assumed these men never left their seats by how easily they fit in with the room's décor, but I recognized a few of their faces from the ceremony.

I didn't remember their names though, and I really hoped that wouldn't come up. Charles was there, I did remember him.

We were down the hall from what was now Alister's office. I hadn't been there since the night with Marley and I wasn't too keen on going back anytime soon.

"President Macavay," one of the men spoke. There was a croaking melody of scraping chairs and creaking bones as the group of men stood in respect. Once Alister was seated, the men returned to their positions as if nothing ever happened.

The formalities of preliminary business started, but the sideways glances I received let me know I'd be the real topic of discussion during that meeting. I sat silently waiting for it to begin.

"As you are aware," the man with the dark brown suit finally said. "There has been some concern raised about your choice of a running mate. Typically, she should have been here at every session and she has not."

I glanced at Alister. "This I was not aware of," I smiled. "I'll make an effort to be present from here on out."

"No," another man coughed. "You wouldn't have been aware seeing as that you've never spent a day in parliament in your life." I could feel the heat rush to my cheeks, but I tactfully stayed silent.

"This is only the second meeting since she has been nominated," Alister said coldly. "And I have already stated, she will need some time to adjust to her new role."

"Perhaps it would be better if…"

"Perhaps nothing," Alister interrupted the man seated across from me. "As per the regulations, it is my right to name my second. Miss Vita is my running mate and there will be no further discussion on this matter."

I looked down at the table. *Great. They all hate me.*

"It is in the interest of this board to have this discussion, President Macavay. Since you have no heir, your position will fall to Miss Vita should anything happen to you. With her questionable past this is cause for concern."

I felt the embarrassment wash over me in waves. The man was right. I had no right to be here. *What were you thinking, Alister?*

"The past is none of your concern," Alister growled. "It is the future we must think of now."

"Ah, but the future is equally concerning," the man retorted. "It is to our understanding that Miss Vita would be beneficial to our cause, but she refuses to use her skills for the greater good."

"What cause?" I whispered to Alister. He shook his head.

"It seems that she doesn't care about the people and that is not a quality that the future president of our country should possess."

"Excuse me?" I laughed. All the men froze and turned toward me. I guess I wasn't supposed to speak. *Oops.*

"Everything you say about me might be true, about my past and the cluelessness to how you do your job, but there is one thing I am certain of…" I paused to study Alister's amused expression. "I have seen the people. Have you? Have you left your ivory tower and walked among your own citizens? I seriously doubt it. The one thing I know to be true above all else is that I genuinely care for people."

Alister put his hand over his mouth to hide his smile. The man across from me turned red.

"And what exactly have you done to show your concern for the people?" he smirked.

"Reynolds, isn't it?" *Hot damn, I remembered his name.* I thought back to my years spent on the broken city sidewalk feeding the Can't Commits.

"Plenty," I smiled. "What have you done?" Reynolds and I held a staring match until the skinny man with a crooked nose at the end of the table spoke.

"Nevertheless, it is in the interest of national security that we must understand Miss Vita's true powers in the realm."

"If she doesn't want to go back there then she doesn't have to." Alister stared at the man with his intense green eyes. "That is final."

"In that case," Reynolds chuckled. "I'm afraid we have no other choice than to require you to produce an heir so the presidency line can continue if something were to happen to you. Fawn, *ahem*, I mean Miss Vita will continue as your second in title because she has been named, but we will vote to change the law allowing her potential reign."

The muscle in Alister's jaw tightened. I looked to Charles and he lowered his bald head. Like pieces of a chessboard, bits of information were used to gain the upper hand. They had to know we were soulmates. I was assuming Charles mentioned this due to the guilty expression on his face. They also must have figured out we didn't want to get married.

Alister chewed his cheek as he calculated the next words to speak. It was like studying how to play a game when all the players were shady assholes.

"Fine." I placed my hands gently on the table. "I will learn more about my powers in the realm. But I will not..." I paused to glare at Reynolds, "Be used. Nor will I use these so-called powers for anything other than what I deem appropriate."

Alister stretched his leg out so it brushed against mine. "Are you sure about this?" he whispered.

"Yes," I answered softly.

"There you have it, gentleman," Alister said. "That is what you have requested and now there will be no more talk on this matter. Unless there is something else to discuss, we are finished here today." He kicked back his chair as he stood, making the dusty old men jump to their feet.

Chapter 3

∞

"Come with me." Alister grabbed my hand and pulled me out the side exit of the building. I glanced back to see the security detail running out of the door just as I slid into the passenger seat of the black Honda waiting in the alley. Alister started the engine and threw the transmission into reverse before peeling out onto the open street.

He raced down the empty roads and I nervously buckled my seatbelt, turning to see if we were being followed. We weren't.

"I take it this isn't allowed?" I asked him breathlessly. Alister shrugged as he gave me a sly smile. He kept the gas pedal pressed to the floorboard.

"Where are we going?" I laughed.

"Where do you want to go? I want to take you on a real date."

"This is your territory. I don't even know what there is to do. Everywhere we used to go back home was in the realm." I thought of Wasters, the bar where Vorie worked until her end of service, and shook my head to erase the painful memories.

"I'm not taking you to the realm," Alister said as he clenched his jaw. "That's the last place you want to be."

"About that," I sighed. "The professor has been begging me to test my powers there for weeks. I'm doing this more for him than for those crusty old men."

Alister grinned. "Thank you for keeping the peace, but let's not talk about that right now. I want it to be just about us today." He turned on the big band music in the car and I held his hand as he drove the winding roads leading us out of the city.

The landscape began to change into towering elms turning orange and red, dotted through with evergreen trees. In between the sturdy trunks, the sun broke through in patches and rolling hills of tall grass appeared like pictures in a moving frame. He drove further into the overgrown country until we came to a large and broken bridge where he parked.

"Is this the ocean?" I gasped, seeing the open expanse of water glittering under the afternoon sun. The bridge once crossed over to what I thought was an island. The water spread out in either direction so far that it seemed to fall off the earth.

"Not really," he smiled. "This is the bay. It's more like a river than the actual ocean."

I thought of the little creek in the mountains that I was so sure was a river and laughed to myself.

"Is the water clean here?" We stepped out of the car and walked down to the shore.

"It's starting to be. They say this water was toxic during the time before the portals. Since then, the natural oyster population has thrived and that is helping to rid the water of the toxins. There was a huge nuclear plant that leaked somewhere in the Pacific Ocean making the coastal water bad there. My great uncle found a way to secure the power plants around here. It's ironic that without humans, the world might actually be a better place," he sighed.

"That's not right," I turned to him. "I've seen the good that people can do. In the mountains, they regulate and use hunting to help manage the wild animal populations. If they didn't do that, overpopulation and disease could run rampant killing off entire species. You can work with the land and take care of it."

"You'll never give up fighting for humankind, will you?" He stared at me as he spoke. "How are you this alive? What happened to make you this way?"

"I don't know," I shrugged. "I've just always wanted to live. What I don't understand is why this is such a rare thing."

"You are amazing." He placed his fingers on the back of my neck and ran his thumb up along my jaw, tilting my face up. Our lips hovered a breath apart and I gently brushed mine against his.

"Can we get in the water?" I asked.

"I don't see why not," he smiled.

I unhooked the snap on my slacks as I kicked off my shoes. Alister's eyes widened as he glanced down to see my pants fall from my waist. I giggled as I pulled off my shirt and tossed it onto his head.

Although it was later in the year, the water was much warmer than the frigid snow fed stream in the mountains. I didn't go very deep, however, because I couldn't see my toes.

"Are you coming?" I turned to ask and laughed when I saw him hurriedly struggling to remove his button-down shirt. His chest was bare as he sauntered toward me. He was definitely in need of some sun, but the lines of his muscles and carved tone of his hips reminded me of the paintings of Greek sculptures.

Blood pumped harder through my veins making me dizzy and breathless. He wrapped his long arms around me and pulled our bodies close together. The cool silt running over my toes and the water lapping at my knees contrasted sharply with the vibration of fire between our skin.

"There are things I'd like to do with you," Alister whispered huskily into my hair. I reached down and splashed him with a large scoop of water.

"You'll have to catch me first."

The sun was sinking lower in the sky as we napped lazily on the sand. I stood and shrugged off Alister's shirt I'd been wearing. My clothes were dirty and wrinkled, but I quickly dressed and piled my knotted hair into a bun on top of my head.

"You're going to have to feed me now." I watched as he slowly pulled on his pants.

"Was that not fulfilling enough?" he smiled seductively.

I rolled my eyes. "I need real food. I'm freaking starving."

As we walked back to the car, Alister raced ahead of me. He climbed onto the hood and reached high up in the branches of the trees stretching over the road, plucking an odd shaped green fruit before jumping down.

"What's this?" I raised an eyebrow as I studied it.

"Food," he grinned. "It's a pawpaw." I bit into the mushy, sickeningly sweet flesh and wiped away the juice that ran down my chin.

"It's interesting," I said. "But I'm going to need a real meal. Why don't we grab a bunch of these to go?" I found a plastic bag in the trunk of his car and we filled it full.

"How did you know about these?" I put the bag in the backseat. "I didn't take you for the kind of guy who can find his own food."

"I know some things," he winked.

We drove back to the city as fast as we'd driven away from it.

"Could we go downtown to the ghetto?" I asked. My stomach was rumbling, and it looked like we'd be too late for dinner at the professor's house tonight. I remembered Freida's street and the vendor ladling out food.

"I'm not sure if that is a safe idea." His tone was flat.

"For me or for you?" I teased. He said nothing. "If you're scared, we don't have to go." I turned to face out the window so he wouldn't see my smile.

"Who says I'm scared?" he asked as he shifted gears.

*

Alister parked the car near the end of the street where Porter picked me up the morning I went to Genie's house. *She's still on her honeymoon,* I remembered. *The letter can wait…*

The ghetto was as vibrant and full of life as it'd been the first time I went there. I grabbed the bag of pawpaws and opened the car door.

"Fawn, wait." Alister put his hand on my arm. "What if they recognize us?"

"So what?" I felt my forehead scrunch in confusion. "These are the people who voted for you. What's wrong if they recognize you?" I brushed off his grip and headed down the street, leaving him to catch up.

The intoxicating smell of food cooking over the open fire pulled me into the waiting line. Alister stood silently beside me, shifting from foot to foot. When we reached the front, I opened the plastic bag for the cook's inspection.

"How many will it cost?" I smiled sweetly.

"For the two of you," she huffed. "The whole bag." I handed her the sack and she ladled a few scoops of noodle soup into two paper bowls, tossing a roll from the bag behind her onto each.

We found an empty spot on the curb and sat down to eat. As I was shoveling food into my mouth, I heard my name being called from somewhere to my right.

"Fawn!" Porter waved me over. He'd just arrived and was setting up his beer stand. "Freida told me you were fine, but I still worried about you."

"You didn't wait long, did you?" I finished the rest of my dinner and threw the bowl into a nearby trash can fire. Alister stood beside me and I laced my fingers reassuringly through his.

"I didn't wait at all. I told you news travels fast." Porter handed Alister and I a cup of beer. "Speaking of that," he lowered his voice. "What are you two doing out here on our dirty street without your entourage, Mr. President?"

"Fawn dragged me here," he smiled. "She's hard to say no to."

"That she is," Porter laughed. Alister held his arm out to pay for the beer.

"None of that," Porter waved him away. "Your credits are no good here and I imagine that the minute I scanned you there would be a swarm of angry guards arriving. You kids just enjoy yourselves and stay out of trouble. Come back for a refill when you're done."

More fires in trash cans were lit and the street musicians began to play. We danced in the shadows on the sidewalk as the crowd swelled in size and grew more animated.

"There should be a way to charge them," a drunken man yelled from his place by one of the fires. "It's not fair for them to expect a free meal just by showing up dying at the portal."

25

"Hang on." I stopped dancing and pulled Alister closer to the loud man's circle. "He's talking about the Can't Commits. I want to hear what he is saying."

"But Johnny's boy still comes back from time to time. He deserves a meal after all he's been through," a woman with a tattered hat and brown jacket puffed a cigar as she responded.

"Aye. Johnny's boy and maybe Gertrude. She did a lot for this area. Can't blame her for wanting to be with her husband," another man said.

"Maybe they should just stay in the realm then," a tall man in a peacoat said as he walked over to join the group. "They don't work for their food. Why should we have to feed them?"

"I agree," the loud man clapped the newcomer on the back. "They should stay here like the rest of us and earn what they get."

"And if they do stay…" The woman blew out a large cloud of smoke. "Would we even have enough to feed ourselves? Half the block leaves in the winter when times get hard. If they all stayed, maybe we wouldn't have enough." The man chugged his beer and tossed his cup into the fire.

"Fawn." The sound of my name caused me to freeze. I closed my eyes in embarrassment.

"Crap," I whispered to Alister before turning around. Freida stood there with scolding eyes and her hands on her hips.

"What do you think you are doing out here?" she asked, her gaze worriedly shifting to Alister. "And with him, nonetheless. Get into my house this instant. The two of you. Go." She pointed sternly at the stairwell across the street and we both lowered our heads as we marched to her door.

"What in the world are you thinking, girl?" Freida glared at me as she fawned over Alister on the couch. He glanced up at the large portrait of Odan hanging in the living room before turning to me with a raised eyebrow. I tried to hide my smile.

"I wanted to show him the real people that he governs," I said softly. "It will make him a better president."

"The Macavays have done just fine without you bossing them around." She narrowed her eyes at me.

Ever the politician, Alister interrupted. "It's not solely her fault, ma'am. I wanted to see how the people really live."

"Well then," Freida huffed as she fell heavily onto the sofa. "What is it you want to know?"

"Who is he?" Alister smiled his charming smile as he motioned toward the portrait.

"That's my boy Odan," Freida gushed. "He's at the Northeast Institute. I've been saving all my life to get him there. He's sharp as a tack, he deserves it."

"What do they learn about at the institute anyway?" I'd never thought to ask it before. Sitting there with Alister, an institute graduate, and Freida so proud of her son, I couldn't help but good-naturedly wonder what was so great about the place.

Alister's face fell as he studied the pattern on the carpet.

Freida beamed, "They learn all about the future of course."

"Their future careers?" I was confused. "Why don't they just study that on the job sites?"

"Nothing like that," Freida scoffed and eyed me like I was slow. "Their eternal futures. They study how to best live out the rest of existence in the realm. The professors help them to discover and advance their true natures so the learning curve of becoming a full-time spirit is less of a struggle."

"They spend their time here in this world studying for the next?" I asked.

"Exactly." Freida clapped her hands together. "Odan will have no problem in his future and he promises to teach me everything he knows. I'm lucky to have such an intelligent and loving boy." She stared fondly at the portrait.

"No offense," I shook my head, "but that's garbage."

"Excuse me?" Her smiled faltered as she turned to me. "I guess I wouldn't expect you to understand given your upbringing."

"No, hear me out," I begged. "Why spend the little time you have in this life shaving a fraction of a second off your eternal life? You have the rest of forever to learn that stuff. Wouldn't time be better spent learning how best to live in this life while you are here?"

"Where do you get such foolish ideas?" Freida chuckled. "What is there to learn here?"

"How to live!" I threw my hands in the air. "And how to make this life better. Maybe if everyone did that, they wouldn't be so quick to leave this world for the realm."

"This life is only temporary," Freida gave me a motherly smile. "The sooner you figure that out, the better off you'll be."

I groaned as I put my head in my hands. "Why does nobody understand?"

"It's the way things are done," Alister said in a distant tone as he walked over to the window. "But Fawn does have a point. What would it take to make your life better, Freida?"

She straightened her skirt and folded her hands in her lap. "My life is just fine, thank you. But since you are asking, Mr. President, maybe a decrease in the institute tuition. Just a little would help to ease the burden. And higher gas rations during the winter. When it gets too cold, we have to power the generators for longer. That makes life difficult here."

"Done." He turned to smile at her.

"Oh, why thank you so much sir," Freida blushed. "I wouldn't have said anything, but you dragged it out of me."

"That I did," Alister laughed. "Now if you'll excuse us, it's getting late and I'd like to take Fawn home."

"Mind your manners," she whispered in my ear as she shoved me toward the door. "And don't let anything happen to that great young president of ours."

*

"What are you thinking?" I asked as Alister maneuvered the car down the darkened city streets.

"I'm glad we went. There are a lot of things I learned tonight and I want to start making some changes."

"Can I help?" I asked in excitement. "I have so many ideas. We should feed the Can't Commits and get more food to the people. Then we should rework the institute to include real life skills like how to work and live and find joy in life. Maybe through art or reading or building. Oh! And we should make them free and everyone should also get free gas and…" My voice trailed off as I realized I was rambling. Alister stared sadly out the window.

"What's wrong?" I cringed. "Too much?"

"Never too much," he smiled at me. "Of course you can help. You're my running mate. I'll see what we can start on tomorrow."

I practically bounced out of the seat as Alister pulled in front of the professor's house. A group of frustrated looking men in suits stood by the front door. Four black sedans screeched forward and boxed in Alister's car.

"I guess my escort is here," he shrugged.

I laughed and quickly kissed him on the cheek. "Thank you for today. I'm so excited to start planning."

I raced up the stairs and past the scolding lectures of the guards before throwing myself happily on top of my giant bed.

Chapter 4

∞

"I'd like to hold our session in the realm today if you are ready." Professor Berlin adjusted the spectacles on his face as he sipped his coffee. I nodded slowly as my heart beat faster. I knew it was inevitable, but I didn't think it would be this soon.

"What exactly are we going to do?" My mouth felt dry and I fought to keep my breathing steady.

"It'll be simple," he reassured me. "My strength in the realm is the ability to focus and I can extend that focus to others. We won't need to go through any grounding points. I'll take us somewhere no one else will be and you can practice your skills. I promise you'll be safe."

"Okay." I bit my lip. "I'm ready."

*

"You don't have to do this if you don't want to." Alister met the professor and me at the portal door. "It doesn't have to be today."

I stiffened as he wrapped his arm around me, fighting the urge to relax into the comforting embrace. He felt my tension and gazed tenderly at me.

"It's okay," he whispered. "We'll do this another time."

"It's no use prolonging the inevitable," I shrugged him off.

"I'm coming with you." He walked beside me to the entrance.

"I don't want you to come." I inhaled deeply as the professor slipped into the void. "I need to do this on my own."

Pain caused his shoulders to sag, but he stepped aside. "I'll wait for you out here," Alister nodded.

With a steady exhale, I touched my arm to the panel, and was sucked through the wave of black all-encompassing nothing.

*

"The first step is the hardest." Professor Berlin stood waiting in the realm as I exited the unfamiliar portal.

"Where are we?" I peered through the shades of gray trying to make out a structure or landmark of some sort.

"Nowhere," he smiled. "This is one of the undeveloped portal exits. It might as well have fallen off the map for all anyone is concerned."

"How are we standing here without floating away?" I asked breathlessly.

"Leave that to me," Professor Berlin chuckled. "I told you that you'd be safe."

"Are you creating gravity?" My eyes were wide.

"No." He tapped his finger against his temple. "I'm focusing to keep us here."

"Don't lose focus then." I took a tentative step toward him.

"Impossible," he said. "First things first, do you recall in your lessons how we've been studying the art of emotional control?"

I nodded, not wanting to speak and distract him from his concentration. *Maybe next time we'll go somewhere with other people. That wouldn't be so bad. At least there would be a platform.* My thoughts were racing.

"Can you control your emotions now?" he asked.

I closed my eyes and met my fear head on. *You trust the professor. He'd have no reason to lie. He knows what he is doing. I'm safe.*

"Better," he smiled. "The art in the realm relies on manifesting your desires. It's paradise here. Whatever makes you happy, you can create. And yet, there are some skills that come more naturally to others based on their dominant traits. You are such an interesting case study because you have so many strong traits. We know you can see through the glamour and that you can destroy. There are other skills that require more souls around, but we will get to those later. For now, I'd like to test a theory. Would you like to give it a try?"

"Do I have another option?" I asked nervously.

"It'll be easy," he promised.

"Okay."

Suddenly, a large boulder appeared in the distance.

"I'd like you to move this rock," he said. "The ability to move someone else's manifestation shows a rare strength of mind."

"I don't know how rare that is." I thought back to my years of servitude. "I've been serving customers manifestations I didn't create for most of my life."

"Ah, but this is different." He crossed his arms. "Those manifestations were designed to move. This one I am purposefully holding in place."

"Maybe you should stop focusing on that and just keep us here instead," I laughed.

"Maybe you should hurry before I exert myself."

I quickly turned to face the rock and pictured it rolling away. Nothing happened. The professor nodded to me encouragingly.

I shifted tactics. Instead I imagined it disappearing and reappearing in a different place. I got a little excited when I saw it vanish, but it came back in the exact same spot.

"Don't try to see through it," he sighed. "Move it."

"What do you think I'm trying to do?" I scoffed as I marched over to the damn thing. *If I can't move it with my mind, I'll move it with my hands,* I thought. I readied myself to push with all my strength as I leaned my shoulder against it. With a low grunt, I shoved hard and immediately fell over as the boulder rolled away as easily as a marble.

"Wonderful," the professor clapped. "I don't think it required the show of brute force, but you'll get better about not needing the physical cues in time. Soon, you will also learn how to hold your own manifestations so that no one else can move them."

"I've never actually created a manifestation before," I grinned sheepishly as I climbed to my feet.

"Never?" He cocked his head to the side. "Have you never tried or never been able to?" I saw

36

the gears spinning behind his eyes as he tried to solve yet another piece of this puzzle and I laughed to myself.

"Never had a reason to," I shrugged.

"Fascinating," he exhaled. "Let's start with something simple." A flowerpot filled with dirt appeared at his feet. "Since you enjoy working in the courtyard so much, manifest a plant. And before you insert your sarcastic comment, yes I noticed." I smiled as I pictured him looking down from his dusty window while taking a break from his studies.

"Alright. Let me try."

I closed my eyes and imagined running my hands through the upturned soil in Fallon's fields. The sun beat down on my back and the smell of fresh earth filled my nostrils. I planted the tiny sunflower seed and watched it sprout. It grew thick and strong. Then the bud opened to reveal beautiful deep golden petals.

"How did you do that?" The professor asked sharply, bringing me out of my trance.

"Do what?" The pot held a perfect sunflower that stood as tall as him. "I made a flower just like you asked. I think it's pretty good," I smiled proudly.

"It's not that." His eyes reflected wide behind his glasses. "You grew the flower. You didn't just manifest it; you actually grew it."

"Um. I'm not sure." I eyed it skeptically. "I just imagined it growing into that."

"Yes. That is what you are supposed to do." He shifted his gaze back to the flower. "But you grew it from a tiny sprout into a full-on mature plant right in front of my eyes. Every detail is exactly perfect. Your first manifestation should have had some holes in it, be flawed in some way. You must see your mistakes and learn from them. Not only did you create a perfect flower, you created every detail through the stages of its life perfectly."

"Well, I've seen it grow so it was easy to remember." I bit my lip as I studied his puzzled face. Laughter bubbled inside of me as his confusion began to make sense.

"No one you know can do that, can they? It's because they haven't seen how things are made. They haven't experienced it themselves and so their manifestations are faulty until they can complete it based off the picture in their minds." I doubled over in a fit of giggles.

"Everything I've been saying is right. Life does have a purpose, even to those of you who want nothing more than to be in the realm. Your eternal paradise is tainted and fake if you never experience life to begin with." I wiped the tears of laughter from my eyes and tried to contain myself when I saw the professor turn red. "I'm sorry. I'm not mocking you. It's just that I've been beating my head against a brick

38

wall trying to get everyone to listen and now I know I'm right."

"I think that's enough for today," Professor Berlin said quietly. "There is much I need to think on. "Can you get rid of this?" He motioned to the flower.

I looked at the beautiful petals and nodded. Placing my hand above it, I willed it away. The amazing thing was that I wasn't angry enough to destroy it, just sad at the thought of leaving it there alone.

*

"How was it?" Alister asked as we exited the portal. The professor waved his hand dismissively as he hurried to his vehicle.

"Not as bad as I imagined," I smiled. "But I think I made him mad." I looked up at Alister's handsome face and reached for his hand. "I'll make it up to him later. There's something I want to start on today."

"Is there a store around here we can go to?" I asked him as he held open the door to the waiting car.

"What kind of store?"

"I need a backpack," I said. Alister raised an inquisitive eyebrow as he told the driver where to go.

"What do you need a backpack for?" he asked as he rolled up the partition window.

"Actually," I laughed. "I'm going to need a lot of backpacks."

*

The supercenter parking lot was as empty as all the ones I'd ever been to. The driver pulled up to the broken glass sliding doors. Years of dust and grime made the entrance floor tacky, but I knew the stuff in the back would be salvageable.

"Bingo," I shouted as I skipped to the racks of dusty hanging bags. Alister pushed a cart with a broken wheel behind me. I began tossing the packs into the basket.

"Why do we need all these?" he asked.

"Because I plan to fill them, of course." He rolled his eyes, but I could tell he was having fun with my mysterious game.

"Let's go to the kitchen supplies." I tugged the edge of the cart. "I want to find those refillable plastic water bottles."

The squeaking cart echoed loudly through the quiet store as I led the way. When the noise of the broken contraption suddenly stopped, I turned to see if he was stuck. Alister leaned his arms on the handle and stared down the aisle of dust covered pinks and blues.

"What is it?" I asked, slightly annoyed at the interruption.

"Nothing." He turned his seductive smile toward me. "Maybe something. I was thinking that one day it'd be nice to have an heir." His eyes traveled slowly down my body.

"Today is not the day," I huffed as I pulled on the cart again. "We have too much work to do."

*

"Where to now, little deer?" Alister asked after we stowed the gear in the trunk.

"We need food."

"How are you always this hungry? There is nothing to you. You can't possibly eat that much," he shook his head as he spoke.

"Not for me," I rolled my eyes. "I need packaged food, and lots of it. Do you know where we can get some?"

*

The warehouse that held the National Food Bank was heavily guarded by barriers and patrols.

"Afraid someone will take something?" I smirked.

"It's our most valuable resource," Alister sighed. "It's been this way for as long as I can remember."

His tracker was scanned twice even though all the guards there called him by his name. A man finally came forward to open the bolted door and we stepped into the giant cement walled building.

"It's freezing in here," I shivered as we walked past the twelve-foot metal shelves filled with boxes.

"Temperature controlled," Alister said.

"I imagine this is what a tomb would feel like." I stared at the expanse of packaged food stretching deeper into the building than I could see from where I stood. There were pallets and cases of various items all neatly labeled and packaged to ship. "Why is all this locked in here? Aren't you afraid it will go bad?"

"No," he shook his head. "We are constantly rotating it when we get new shipments."

"I don't understand." There was a package marked 'energy bars' and I pulled it down from the shelf. The man behind us noted the selection on a clipboard.

"It's a little complicated," he said. "But I'll try my best to explain. You see, the farmers work for the government and we have control of where their products go. The mafia owns the processing plant, so we give some food to them in exchange for packing food for us. The oil fields are neutral, but we pay them in food for our fuel. The mafia owns the tracking system mostly and hoards the portal technology..."

He paused briefly to motion to a box of canned chicken and I saw a bitter smile play on his lips. I hastily pulled the package down while the man behind us took his notes.

"They've had the portal system science since the beginning," he continued. "Since the technology went wide. We've never been able to duplicate it once they took the files. We have our scholars though, and the mafia sends their children to our institutes. And we both have techs operating the cell phone towers which makes the tracking system available to all of us on a limited data platform. Our servers are able to access it, and keep us connected, but the maintenance belongs to the mafia."

"I'm still confused." I turned to him.

"The system is complicated," he sighed.

"Not about that," I shook my head. "Well, a little about that, I guess. I want to know how the government owns the farmers. They seem to be the ones doing all the work. Shouldn't they own themselves?"

"They chose this." He gave me a condescending smile that made my cheeks flush. "They voted to utilize our services, sending aid in time of need and transporting goods for them, plus providing a level of protection against the mafia and other consumers. Where would they be without us?"

"Probably rich," I muttered under my breath, thinking of Fallon and his surplus of food.

"This is your credits then?" I asked out loud, looking at the boxes towering above my head.

"Something like that," Alister smiled. "We all use the credit system, mafia and government included, just think of this as a back up to the credit. A sort of National Reserve Bank."

Chapter 5

∞

Alister and I sat in the foyer of the professor's house beneath the worn and faded paintings. The guards begrudgingly carried over filled water bottles from the kitchen under Freida's watchful eye. We had an assembly line of packs before us which we filled with basic hygiene items, easy to open foods, and the water containers.

"Now, tell me what this is for," Freida said as she crouched down on the floor to help us. Alister shook his head and sighed as he zipped up another bag.

"It's for the Can't Commits," I laughed. "The portal jumpers or whatever you call them out here. That way their bodies can heal, and the people won't struggle to feed them."

"And how are the weak ones supposed to feed themselves?" she asked.

"That's part two of my plan," I winked.

"I thought we agreed that winking isn't a good look for you," Alister chuckled. I tossed an energy bar at his head.

*

We spent the next few days driving around to every active portal within a hundred-mile radius that we could access. The hardest part was finding someone who promised to check for the Can't Commits that would need help feeding themselves.

Alister offered twenty credits a day to those who would help and that finally got us enough interest. We left the bags outside the portals with makeshift signs for the incomers.

"This will work short term." Alister draped his arm over my shoulder after we'd dropped off the last pack. "But we need to come up with a more sustainable plan."

"Working on it," I sighed as I dragged him back to the vehicle.

*

The professor had been distant and distracted after our session in the realm. As we sat at the dinner table, I watched him study his books intently while his food remained untouched.

"I didn't mean to upset you." I put my fork down on my empty plate and crossed the room to stand near him.

"Upset me?" He looked up from his book. "Why on earth would you think that?"

"We haven't had any more sessions lately," I shrugged. "And you've been a bit preoccupied."

"I've been busy learning." He touched his forehead and smiled. "You've given me a lot to think about. Speaking of learning, how are you doing with your government studies?"

I pulled out the chair next to him and sat hugging my knees to my chest. "Good, I think. I've been experimenting with practical application lately. Trying to start some new programs for the people."

"Always the activist," he smiled warmly.

"Is that what I am?" I laughed. "If you say so, it must be true."

"I don't know about that." His smile faltered. "What do Alister and the board think about your new altruistic endeavors?"

"Alister approves," I nodded. "We will bring it up with the board at the monthly meeting."

"I see," Professor Berlin yawned. "Well, whatever they decide, just know your heart is in the right place."

*

I'd found new music at the store with the backpacks. New to me at least. Punk rock wasn't something I'd picked up before, but the beats were invigorating. No one makes music like this anymore. Don't get me wrong, I adore the solo instruments and small bands playing folk songs or sweet melodies where people gather. And there was a concert in the realm Genie dragged me to one time, but I wanted to be somewhere real where I could really see the musicians in my earbuds.

As I laid on the carpeted floor next to my bed thinking about how to organize a music festival of some sort, I felt the air shift around me. A cold breeze nipped the end of my nose before settling on my chest causing me to shiver. I reached up to turn off the music. Pushing myself up to a seated position, I glanced around the silent room.

"Who's there?" I whispered to no one.

Suddenly, the ghostly outline materialized right before my eyes sitting cross-legged on the rug in front of me.

"You didn't sing this time." I put my hand over my heart. "I wasn't sure it was you."

"Your headphones were in. I didn't want to waste my breath," Vorie smiled.

"I wish I could hug you right now," I said. "Life has been so crazy lately and I missed you these past few days."

"I'm sorry sweetie. There's been some new stuff to learn and I haven't had time to visit. But I was thinking you should come see me in the realm now that you have a tracker again."

"About that," I glared at her. "Why didn't you tell me Marley was going to hold me down and put it in? And this second in command thing? A little warning would have been nice."

"But then you would have run and never fulfilled your destiny," she giggled.

"Is this my destiny then?" I fought the smile aching to curl my lips.

"Maybe," she said. "You know I'm not a psychic."

"Um. You can see stuff coming that I can't." I leaned back on the palms of my hands. "Is this the life I'm meant to live or not?"

"Right now?" She looked around the room. "Yes. This is exactly where you are supposed to be."

"And what do you mean by right now?"

"Exactly what I said." Her eyes were playful as she turned to me.

"I wish you'd stop being so evasive and just give me a straight answer."

"I can't help it," Vorie shrugged. "I'm a ghost."

"Right." I rolled my eyes. "Okay. I'm going to the realm. I want to see the paradise you've created. When is a good time to visit?"

"How about this weekend?" A beautiful smile brightened her face. "Genie is coming back from her honeymoon. She and Craton are going to Dives on Saturday."

"Should we all go? You didn't get to…" My voice trailed off as I remembered the vivid details of that night. "Would you want to go?" I asked softly.

"No," she shook her head laughing. "I don't want to go, but I would love it if you came to see where I live. Feel free to bring Alister too. Then you can go to Dives after."

"You know, I'm not really sure I want to go there either. Maybe we'll just come see your place and leave. I'm not too big on the realm still."

"I know," she said. "I hated it too. But you need to go to Dives. It's all a part of your journey."

"Is there more to this journey? I don't know if I can take any more surprises."

Vorie smiled. "So much more, but you'll be alright. I'll give away one little secret though. Expect a letter from Genie tomorrow."

*

"I have something for you," Freida said as I walked behind her. I went to the sink and began to clean the dirt from under my nails. "It's on the counter there." She pointed with her kitchen knife.

"A letter?" I pretended to act surprised. *Maybe Vorie telling me things took the joy from the discovery…*

Freida eyed me curiously. "Yes. A letter from Virginia." She pushed me toward the door. "And I have scones for your breakfast today so don't be late."

*

I'm telling you it was amazing! We walked through the ruins of Paris. You know, the place all those Vogue magazines said fashion started. I found the cutest dress in an abandoned boutique. Gosh, I'm still crying that I had to leave it behind. There were sequins and feathers all over it. It was perfect!

Craton promises to get me something exactly like it designed in the realm. Then we portal hopped to Italy and stayed at this sweet little inn. We helped make wine with our freaking feet! Can you believe it?

I can't wait to tell you all of this in person. Vorie says you have a tracker again, Miss Vice President or whatever we are calling you now. Say you'll meet us at Dives this weekend. We can make it a double date!

xoxoxo

Your best alive friend

I smiled as I clutched the letter to my chest. Genie's enthusiasm always won me over. I hastily scribbled a reply saying I wouldn't miss it for the world and Freida agreed to drop it off with Porter that evening.

"I think we should go back to the realm today," Professor Berlin said after breakfast. "There are some things I'd like to study more."

"I'm actually going to the realm on Saturday," I laughed. "Genie wants to meet at Dives and I'm going to see Vorie's place."

"Have you spoken with Alister about this yet?" The professor glanced nervously at the table.

"Why would I need to speak with him?" I asked in confusion. "I'm sure he won't mind. This is what you all wanted, isn't it? Me to go back to the realm. Well I'm going, so be happy."

"There's more to it than that," he sighed. "We have to make sure it's safe."

"This isn't happening again," I groaned as I put my head in my hands. "I'm going to see my friends. I'll take Alister and whatever amount of guards needed with me. How much danger can I be in?"

"It's not just your safety I'm worried about," he smiled. "It's everyone else's too."

"What?" I lifted my face. "I'm not going to hurt anyone."

"Let's discuss this in the realm today. Then you must promise to speak with Alister before going to Dives this weekend."

*

We entered through the portal static and the void spit us out in the same place where I'd grown the sunflower. I stared wistfully at the empty space where it once was.

"I want you to try something for me." Professor Berlin stood with his arms crossed. "I want you to manifest some glamour."

"That's impossible." I raised my arm that held the tracker beneath the scars. "This thing limits our abilities."

"For most people this is true," he grinned. "But not for all. Let's see if you can do it."

"I'll give it a shot," I shrugged. I'd never really cared about glamour before, so it was hard to imagine what I'd want. Thinking of Genie's letter reminded me about the beautiful black silk gown I'd found for our first trip to Dives. I could feel the material slipping over my fingers, and I smiled at the memory of Vorie telling me to get it despite Genie's choice of the itchy green one.

"Amazing," the professor whispered. I opened my eyes and looked down at the flowing fabric of my favorite dress that was wrapped around my body.

"How is it possible?" I gasped. "Could I have done this the whole time? What about the trackers?"

53

"There is more to the technology than you think." He stared at me intently. "The control for these devices comes from a mixture of science and what we would consider magic."

"Magic? Like spells and witches?" I laughed.

"This isn't a joke." His voice was sharp, and my smile dropped off my face. "When humanity learned there were forces at work in the universe with magical elements that could be manipulated by these so-called witches, scientists set out to study it. The portal technology resulted from this research. Unfortunately, when the mafia stole the technology and leaked it to the general public, everyone left, and the research was left unfinished."

"Am I a witch or something?" His seriousness was frightening. I'd never seen him this way.

"No. You are not. A witch is someone who seeks out and practices the art of magic. You are just an unnaturally stubborn and very alive woman, because of this you are able to do things ordinary people can't."

"Like make glamour without using a tracker?" I asked.

"For some reason, you can bypass the limiting spells on the neocortex of your brain that the tracker emits. There are many theories as to how some people can do that, but I suspect that the strength of your imagination is somehow stronger than others too. This is why you were able to destroy the magical grates at The Nocere."

My head was spinning, and I quickly manifested a bench to sit on. *Magic, witches, spells...* Somehow this all made sense and yet it seemed too farfetched to grasp.

"I wish I knew what to call you," the professor said as he came to sit next to me. "This is why the study is necessary. We have to learn all you can do and how you are able to do it."

"Wouldn't it be possible to speak with some of the spirits from the past? The scientists or someone?" I asked hopefully. "Maybe they'd know more than us."

Professor Berlin looked sadly out over the gray expanse of the realm. "I wish it was that easy. However, it seems they no longer care for the world. Their time in it has passed and there is no one living to draw them to it. They are unreachable living in their own paradises."

I thought of Vorie still tethered to us and unable to distance herself. My heart broke for her, but I was selfishly glad she didn't disappear.

"But I believe you are the key to learning more about the universe," he continued. "There has to be a bigger reason for why you possess such a wide array of skills when no one else does."

"Professor." I reached for his hand. "I don't think there is. You shouldn't get your hopes up chasing theories. I honestly believe everyone could have these skills if they just practice and live their lives to the fullest."

He patted the top of my hand and smiled sympathetically. "We'll see."

Chapter 6

∞

The yellow leaf curled from the cooling air and drifted lazily down from the tree above me. I watched it fall as I sat on the cold stone bench. It landed softly in front of my feet. The water fountain was empty, and I studied it, devising a way to make it work again so the birds could drink from it in the spring. The door from the house opened, breaking my train of thought.

"I was hoping you'd come today." I smiled as Alister stepped onto the walkway. His slow saunter and sultry grin caused my pulse to quicken. "I need one of those phone things so I can summon you at my command."

Alister bit his bottom lip. "No need to summon me, I'm always at your command."

"Whatever," I rolled my eyes. "Come sit down. I need to talk with you."

"Talk first?" He took a seat beside me and reached out to brush his thumb along my chin.

"Yes talk." I clasped his hand between the two of mine despite the fire spreading down my neck. "Genie is back from her honeymoon. I want to go see her at Dives this weekend. It'll be a double date with us and her with Craton. Oh, and I want to see Vorie's paradise beforehand. What do we need to do to make this happen?" I felt his muscles tense and I scooted closer, so our legs were touching.

"Please," I begged, giving my best doe eyes. "I'll do anything."

"Anything?" he smirked.

"Oh geez. Get ahold of yourself," I sighed as I dropped his hand. "I meant whatever the rules are about going out. I'll do that."

"Hey," he laughed. "I was only teasing. Whatever makes you happy is what we'll do. I'll work out the details to get you there. I promise."

*

The next day dragged on forever. At the appointed hour of Alister's arrival, I stood nervously watching through the window. Something about the way he tensed when I asked to go had me worried that he wouldn't show up. The black sedans rolled onto the street at precisely 6 o'clock. I released a tense breath in a steady exhale and called good-bye to Freida.

"You look beautiful tonight," Alister said as he motioned for the driver to stay seated and held the door open for me himself.

"Oh, this old thing?" I giggled as I slowly turned around. "Some handsome stranger picked it out for me a long time ago and hung it in my closet."

"I knew it would look great on you," he whispered in my ear. "Now let's go see your friends."

*

The hallway we entered was almost identical to the one in LA I'd used my whole life. Except the glamour for sale was more intricate than any I'd ever seen. I pictured Genie gawking at these windows and smiled. There were entire body suits of different animals, moving and breathing gowns in every shade of imaginable color, and holographs lining an entire wall.

"Do you want anything?" Alister held my hand as I studied the sweet little birds dancing around a metal cage skirt.

"No," I shook my head. "Let's just go see Vorie."

She was waiting for us outside of the hall. I rushed forward to wrap my arms around her and laughed as I felt her solid body under the embrace. No ghostly outline, no wisps of essence. It was just Vorie in the flesh. *Well, in the spirit, I guess.*

There was something slightly different about her. She looked older in some way. Her skin was paler and the air around her was still. Her eyes were so deep and distant that I suddenly felt uncomfortable.

"Come on." Vorie suddenly smiled her beautiful smile and I forgot why I was hesitant. "I can't wait to show you where I live."

We locked arms and manifested to the base of a large mountain. I gasped when I saw the pine trees.

"Is this what I think it is?" I turned to her with my mouth agape.

"Yep," Vorie laughed. "Welcome to my version of Idaho."

The two guards that came with us hung back as we started down the path through the grassy field.

"I'll stay here too," Alister said. "Go spend some time with your friend." I kissed him gratefully on the cheek and followed Vorie into her paradise.

The flora she'd created hauntingly reminded me of the Ruby Mountains, but there were slight differences in the greenery and terrain. We continued past a crystal-clear lake and the brightness of the sun was quickly replaced with the reflection of the moon on the water.

"I'm still working on the details of this part during the day." She grabbed my hand as she pulled me along. "You can check this out later when I'm finished."

The path led through a towering forest thick and full. The birds that danced around the branches chirped with sweet piano notes.

"I've been playing around with their sounds," she told me when I stopped to listen. "I got the idea from you when you saw the birds in the mountains."

She laced her arm through mine as we crossed a wooden bridge. A flower covered gazebo and stone path led us to a tiny cabin nestled in the trees.

Once we were inside, I was transported home again. Well, home to Vorie's flat in the city. Tears gathered in my eyes. The giant windows with sheer curtains, her comfortable couch, and the muted hues of blue décor scattered artfully around. Everything was there.

"You're not saying much," she nudged me.

"It's all so perfect and beautiful." My lip began to quiver.

"Oh, don't cry," she cried out as she reached over to hug me.

"You don't cry," I sniffled. "If you cry, I'll never be able to stop." We both inhaled deeply and burst into laughter mixed with tears.

"Ah. Okay," I exclaimed as I wiped my eyes. "I'm alright now." I turned to look at the bookshelves that mirrored the ones Brayson had lovingly built for her.

"I expected the library to be a little more grandiose than this," I teased.

"Just wait and see." She pushed me forward.

As we stepped up to the bookshelf, the wall suddenly expanded, and we were standing in a room as large as the professor's house. Shelves lined the walls from floor to ceiling filled with a colorful assortment of books. A stone fireplace was surrounded by seating pillows strewn across the floor. A giant bay window with a plush bench seat lit up the entire room.

"This is amazing," I whispered as my eyes opened wider to take it all in. "I can't believe you've read this many books."

"I haven't." Her face cringed in embarrassment. "Most of these are blank, but I liked the way they looked. I was thinking that I could maybe write my own stories in them one day."

"I can't wait to read them," I smiled. "Wait! Let me give you these. I just finished them from the professor's library." I manifested some of the fiction books I'd read lately and gave them to her. She took them gratefully and skimmed through the pages as I ran my finger along the titles on the shelf.

"I haven't read this one," I said as I pulled a beautiful red book from the stack.

"Maybe later," Vorie laughed as she tugged me back through the expanding wall. "Let me make you some tea."

I let myself sink comfortably into the oversize couch as she carried over the tray. I caught the slightest whiff of my favorite herbal brew, but the taste still wasn't there.

"Don't worry," she said. "It tastes different when you are here full time." I pulled the large knit blanket over our laps and leaned back against the cushion.

"This is why they all left, isn't it?" I asked. "Maybe the realm isn't all that bad. Sure, what we've dealt with so far sucks, but I could stay here with you forever."

Vorie placed her teacup on the tray. "One day, you will. We will all be together. But for now…" she whispered the words and we were back at the beginning of the path that led through the forest.

"Why'd you do that?" I groaned once the shock wore off. "I was just getting comfortable."

"Too comfortable." Vorie nudged me with her shoulder. "It's not your time. I don't want you here until then. Plus, Genie will freak out if you don't show up."

"I know," I sighed. "It just felt so nice to be home."

"It's not your home yet," she smiled. "You still have work to do."

*

The crowd at Dives was overwhelming. There was a hazy blur of amber colored lights and falling autumn leaves from darkened branches on the ceiling. Dripping wax candles flickered on the tables. Fall glamour was in full swing with ghoulish monsters and elaborate costumes on all the patrons. I laced my fingers through Alister's fingers to ground myself.

"Are you alright?" he whispered against my hair as he drew me closer to him.

"Yes," I nodded. "It's just so loud. I almost forgot what it's like up here."

"Focus on what's real," he said. I took a steadying breath and willed it all away.

We were standing in the vast expanse of nothing flanked by the guards in their blue suits. The people in the club wore simple clothes and spoke to one another in loud voices as they fought to be heard over the manifested music. It was comical really, everyone standing or sitting in thin air, fooled by the illusions.

I scanned the crowd and looked over to where the bar should be. An old man, naked as a newborn baby, stood speaking with the bartender.

"Oh my gosh," I giggled as I pointed him out to Alister.

"It happens more often than you'd think," he laughed. "They get their kicks that way. Since there are so few of us that can see through the glamour like we can, they never get caught."

"Aaahhh!"

I heard her squeal from behind me and the glamour came back into place when I lost focus. Genie threw her arms over my shoulders and the guards rushed forward to help.

"It's fine guys." I held up my hand. "This is my friend."

Genie rolled her eyes as she looked at them. "Did they have to come?"

"They'll hang back," I reassured her. "Now let me look at this dress."

She stepped away and raised her arms in the air as she posed for me to admire it. Little feathers adorned the top and waist of the gown. The sequins on the bodice were so closely woven together that they reflected the floating lights as she moved. The waist fell and ended with longer feathers so black that they shone with every color.

"You look like a crow," I gasped. Genie's eyes narrowed. "A beautiful crow," I quickly smiled. "This dress was made for you."

I knew I was forgiven for my poor word choice when she placed her arm through mine. As she pulled me away, I turned to see Alister giving Craton a cold and businesslike handshake.

"What's that about?" I asked Genie.

"Who cares?" she laughed. "Tonight isn't about them. It's about us having fun. Promise you'll drink with me." Alister turned to look at me and his eyes lit up. *Maybe I just imagined the tension.* I shook my head.

"Of course I'm drinking," I smiled at her. "What are we starting with?"

Craton and Alister got our orders from the bar and Genie rehashed the details of her honeymoon that she'd outlined in the letter. Her enthusiasm made me giddy and I kept having flashbacks to our years spent together in our flat in LA.

When the guys came back with our drinks, they sat on either side of us silently watching the conversation. The discomfort between the two of them became so palpable that even Genie noticed it.

"Dance with me?" she turned to ask Craton after she'd downed her drink.

"Always." He smiled adoringly at her as they walked to the ballroom floor. I waved away her request to join them while laughing and turned to Alister once they were gone.

"What's with you tonight?" I asked.

"Nothing," he said. "Are you having a good time?"

"I am, but you don't seem like you are. Do you not like Craton for some reason?" I crossed my arms as I leaned back in my chair, studying his face for an explanation.

"He seems like a decent enough guy," Alister shrugged. "You know my feelings on the mafia though. His father has a prominent role and has been at odds with the government for years."

"Maybe you should get to know him," I said. "He is nothing like his father. I actually think he'd be on board with some of the changes you'd like to make in the future."

Alister leaned forward and gently kissed me on the cheek. "Look at you being a devious politician."

My face grew hot. "There is nothing devious about it. You want change, then look for the people that will help you make it happen."

"Unfortunately, the world isn't so black and white, little deer," he sighed. "But if you trust him, I promise to make more of an effort to connect."

"Thank you." I smiled triumphantly before looking around the room. Two men wearing pinstripe suits came walking through the arched doorways with a beautiful girl between them. Her bright red hair was long and flowing with fire burning from the tips. I half gasped, half shrieked.

"What is it?" Alister followed my gaze to the newcomers. "Is that…"

"Lilith!" I screamed. She turned to the sound of her name being called and squealed happily when she saw me. Leaving the two suitors at the door, she raced over to my table. I wrapped my arms around her in a tight embrace.

"Fawn," she gushed as she squeezed me back. "I'd heard you were okay, and that you were some government big wig now too, but I still was so worried about you. Are you alright?"

"I'm good," I smiled as I released my grip. She'd changed somehow, either she'd filled out more or her hair was longer. I couldn't put my finger on it, but she was still just as beautiful. I noticed the stolen glances at her from the men in the room.

"How are you?" I shook my head in disbelief. I couldn't believe she was standing right in front of me. "Have you seen the girls? How are they?"

"Oh mate, it's been a long year. Chloe and Claire finished their service. They are starting this bar up in New York where they are from, and they've taken like a fairy godmother role to this little girl from the orphanage."

"Sammy?" I asked breathlessly.

"I think that's her name," Lilith nodded. "And Astrid disappeared a few weeks ago if you can believe it. We stayed in contact pretty regularly, but just like that, she was gone." She leaned in close to whisper in my ear, "I think she cut her tracker out."

My mind was racing with all this new information. I had to find a way to get in touch with Juniper. *Maybe she found her...*

"I haven't gotten in touch with Fergus. Rumor has it he is working somewhere in Virginia," she continued, "And Karl is back in England. I don't know where Bemouth went."

"It's so awesome to see you and to hear how everyone is doing." I hugged her again. "How are you though? Is your contract up?"

"It is," she laughed.

"What are you doing for work now?" I looked down at the red dress she was wearing, it was one of the more expensive ones in the glamour display.

Her cheeks turned a bright pink, making her look even more alluring. "I kind of learned this sweet trick. Do you want to see?"

"Sure." I looked down at Alister. He seemed to be avoiding our conversation, but the way he studied his beer glass let me know he was listening.

Lilith straightened her shoulders and raised her chin. She gently bit her bottom lip and curled a paint tipped finger toward the two men she'd entered Dives with. They tripped over one another as they rushed to her. I watched in absolute fascination as an old man in their path stood absentmindedly while staring at Lilith and seemingly regained his sense before sitting at his table again. The two suitors with chiseled jaws stood drooling at her side.

"Would you two mind getting me a drink?" she asked sweetly. The men raced to the bar. I clasped my hand over my mouth as I watched the scene unfold.

"Are you controlling them with magic or something?" I asked.

"I don't know what it is," she laughed. "It's been fun though."

I shook my head in awe. "Well come sit down with us." I pulled out a chair for her.

"I wish I could," Lilith pouted. "But we are only staying for a moment. I promised some friends that I'd meet them at Shoulgans, but I wanted to pop in here for a quick drink first."

"Oh, okay." I stared at her sadly. For some reason I had the overwhelming urge to beg her to stay. "Don't be a stranger. Stay in touch."

"You too." She blew me a kiss as she walked away. I watched her shoes click across the floor and remembered the fire at The Nocere.

"She's a siren." Alister's voice pulled me from my trance. "An untrained one nonetheless."

"What?" I turned to face him. I didn't know how long I'd been standing there staring and instantly felt embarrassed. When I looked back to the bar, Lilith and her escorts were gone.

"A siren is someone who emits sexual energy as their dominant trait," he explained. "I was able to block her out, but only barely. She'll be very powerful someday with the right training and practice."

I sat heavily in my chair, feeling drained from the interaction. "Did you think she was beautiful?"

"Not as beautiful as you are." He placed his hand gently on top of mine and I rolled my eyes. Genie dragged Craton off the dance floor while laughing. Alister stood and changed seats to sit closer to him.

"Oh, thank God," Genie excitedly whispered to me. "I just told my darling husband that if he didn't make friends with your man, I'd start speaking my mind to his mother."

Chapter 7

∞

As the night wore on, we continued to talk and drink while the crowd at Dives became more animated. The monstrous costumes of the guests grew more vibrant and elaborate with every passing hour.

After a round of shots, I dragged Alister to the dance floor. The alcohol wasn't affecting me, but the noise and lights were making me dizzy. I laid my head against his chest as we swayed to the haunting melody of the song.

"Are you ready to go?" he asked gently. I peeked out from the folds of his shirt to see Craton spinning Genie around the middle of the room.

"A few more minutes," I smiled as I snuggled closer to him. When the song was over, Genie grabbed my hand and pulled me to the bar.

"One last drink," I laughed. "Then we have to get going."

She pushed out her bottom lip, but a quick glance through the perfect glamour makeup showed her eyes were as tired as I felt so I knew she wouldn't argue much. We reached the crowded bar counter and I held our place while she skipped over to get the bartender's attention. I leaned against the ornate wood carved counter and rested my hand on my chin as I looked at the shining mirror reflecting the amber lights and branches on the ceiling.

"Tsk. Tsk," a man's voice whispered from behind me. The sound sent a freezing chill through my veins. "What is the little orphan girl doing here all alone?"

His scarred hand slid onto the bar beside me and I could make out the vague imprint from where I'd bit him as a child. My heart beat so loudly in my ears that it drowned out the sounds from the rest of the room.

"It's Miss Vita now." My voice sounded so much stronger than I felt. I straightened my shoulders to match it. I turned to face the shadow monster, the bastard who killed my friend, and bile rose in the back of my throat. "I don't think I ever got your name." I narrowed my eyes coldly at him.

"Still have the fight in you it seems." The monster smiled with his gleaming teeth. "Kingston," he said, holding his hand out for me to shake.

I felt my stomach roll as he said his name and left his hand hanging in the air. "I'm not comfortable touching monsters who prey on children and kill innocent women."

"Still no manners, I see." He shook his head.

73

I glanced quickly around the room. Alister was laughing at something Craton said, but when our eyes met, he jumped up from his seat.

"I've got our drinks," Genie giggled as she bumped into me. Her laughter faded when she looked at my face.

"Who is this?" she asked, turning to see the monster. He glanced nervously to her and anger turned my vision red.

"Don't you dare look at her!" I screamed. The glass Genie had placed in my hand disintegrated as I clenched my fist.

"Is that him?" Genie asked worriedly as she felt the anger rising from me.

"Yep," I snarled as I glared at him. "That's the coward who killed Vorie." Kingston stepped backward but he didn't get a chance to manifest away before Genie lunged at him screaming.

The rage was overwhelming, and I felt the room shake around me. The branches snapped from the ceiling and I could hear the bottles clinking on the shelves. *Politics be damned.* I rushed forward like the little orphan I was to help my friend kick the monster's ass.

We managed to get him to the ground. Genie and I both swung blindly at his head. Too soon, I felt Alister lift me by my waist.

"It's him," I screamed through angry sobs. "That's the guy who did it." Craton was holding Genie back by her arms and pulling her towards the door.

"Calm down, little deer," Alister whispered in my ear. "This place is falling apart."

I looked over at the shattered mirror above the bar and gasped. I hadn't meant to do that. The guards were at our side two seconds later. Somehow this had all happened before they could get there. *What were they even here for?*

"You have to breathe," Alister said as he dragged me to the exit. The room felt unnaturally hot. I inhaled deeply to calm myself down.

"Get those two out of here," a bouncer yelled from somewhere to my right.

"I'm trying," Alister said coldly. I chanced a final glance at the monster before I left the room. A man was standing over him with an outstretched hand to help Kingston up. He looked to me curiously, a smile forming on his lips. *Reynolds.*

"You've got to be kidding me!" I tried to lunge forward again, but Alister picked me up and carried me through the door. Genie was clawing at Craton, screaming to be let go. I don't know how they did it, but they managed to manifest us to the hall.

Genie and I held hands as we slid down shaking against the wall. We sat on the floor and Genie kicked off her shoes. Neither of us spoke.

"Are you okay, sweetheart?" Craton asked, breaking the awkward silence. She stared blankly ahead. The government guards materialized at the door.

"Where the hell were you?" Alister growled.

"Probably taking care of Reynolds." I glared at him. The men looked anxiously at their feet and I could see the fear of losing their livelihood by the defeat in their stance.

"It's not their fault," I sighed as I stood up and pulled Genie to her feet. "We told them to give us some space."

"You should have been paying attention," Alister's voice was a sharp whisper.

"Just let it go." I shook my head.

"Let what go?" Genie suddenly shrieked. "How does that bastard get away with something like this? He needs to be punished. Where does he live? I'll go murder him myself."

Craton wrapped his arm around her. "I'll find him, and I'll take care of this. I've seen his face before. He's one of the mafia's tech guys that works with the portal system. I'll make him disappear." Genie relaxed against Craton as he spoke.

"I'll help," Alister said coldly. "If he has connections in the government, then his position must be pretty high up. You'll need my assistance for this." Alister and Craton looked at each other with a newfound respect.

"And what exactly are you going to do?" I stared at the three of them in disbelief. "If you kill him, what does that solve? He'll just go to the realm and live out the rest of his existence in peace." I kicked the manifested wall with the heel of my shoe. "I hate this stupid place."

"We have to do something." Genie looked at me with angry tears in her eyes. "We have to avenge Vorie."

"I'm fine." Vorie suddenly manifested next to us in the hallway. The guards stepped forward and Alister raised his arm to hold them back.

"She is not the threat tonight," he snapped.

"We will get him for you," Genie sobbed against Vorie's shoulder. "I'll strangle him with my bare hands."

"I believe you would." Vorie lifted Genie's chin up as she smiled at her. "But he doesn't deserve your tears. Let it go for now. These things have a way of working themselves out."

Her ethereal smile and loving embrace caused my lip to quiver. "Are we just supposed to pretend it never happened?"

"Yes," she laughed. "He's nothing more than a cockroach and he is afraid of you." She looked knowingly into my eyes. "Keep doing what you are doing. There are bigger things to worry about than this."

*

I slumped weakly into the backseat of the sedan and curled up against Alister as the car drove us away from the portal.

"Are you alright, little deer?" he asked as he wrapped his arm around me.

"I will be in the morning." My heart and voice felt deflated. "Will you stay with me tonight?"

*

The sun was shining through the window when I awoke the next morning. The spot where Alister slept was empty, but I could still smell him on the pillow. I hugged it to my chest, relishing in the comforting scent.

"Good morning, deer." The door swung open and Alister carried in a tray of food.

"I thought you left," I said as I quickly sat up and wrapped the sheet around my naked chest. The reflection from the vanity mirror gave me a glimpse of my unruly hair and I ran my fingers through it the best I could.

"I wouldn't leave without feeding you," he winked. "Although I'm not sure that Freida approves of you entertaining male visitors in your room."

"Ah." I crinkled my nose in embarrassment. "She wasn't rude to you, was she?"

"No." Alister smiled as he set the breakfast tray on the bed. "But I get the feeling you are in for a lecture soon." I reached hungrily for the food as Alister slowly sipped his coffee.

"What are we going to do about Reynolds?" I asked between bites of toast.

"Unfortunately, I don't think there is much I can do. The cabinet appointments are not made by me, but by the people." He looked bitterly out the window. "Technically, he hasn't done anything wrong. The back-door deals and alliances formed go back generations between government and mafia. It makes me sick. I'm tired of the corruption."

"But Craton isn't that bad." I looked to him hopefully.

"No, he isn't." The smile returned to his face. "The whole political system is a mess."

"Nothing is black and white," I reminded him.

"It'd be good if you take that advice too," he smirked.

"How do we fix it all?" I pushed the tray aside and cuddled next to him.

"Slowly." Alister rubbed my shoulder. "We'll start with the meeting tomorrow."

*

"The mirror broke when you were angry?" Professor Berlin asked as we stood in the forgotten portion of the realm. "And you didn't touch it?"

"No. I already told you that." I manifested a reclining chair and sank down into the thick cushions. The professor had been questioning me for what seemed like an hour already. "It just cracked when I felt the air shake."

"And you didn't consciously will it to shake or break?"

I shook my head. "I didn't have time to think of anything else. I was just scared and angry and hurt."

"Which of these emotions was dominant at the time?"

"All of them," I shrugged.

"Fascinating." The professor began to pace. "I had theorized that you feel things so strongly at any given moment and are able to tap into different abilities. But now it seems that you feel a multitude of different things and this somehow causes the realm to become unstable."

"The whole realm?" I asked wide-eyed.

"Not the whole thing I'm sure, but the manifestations around you can't withstand the energy you emit at certain times."

Well good, I thought smugly. *The realm doesn't like me as much as I don't like it.*

"Wait." I scooted to the edge of the deep chair. "Does this mean I can tap into any ability? Can I be a siren too?"

Professor Berlin stopped pacing and arched an eyebrow in my direction. "Why on earth would you want to do that?"

"No reason," I blushed. "I just want to know what I am capable of."

"Don't we all." His expression was a mixture of deep thought and confusion, leaving me to wonder what he meant.

"Is there something you're not telling me?"

"What makes you think that?" His eyes suddenly focused behind his glasses.

"Just a feeling."

"It might be a good idea for you to tame the feelings down for the foreseeable future," he snapped.

"Alright. I'll work on it. What would you like me to practice on today?" I asked, trying to redirect his mood.

"I think that's enough for today," he sighed. "In light of this new information, I feel it's best to postpone our sessions until I can study this further."

*

I wanted to check the portals on our way to the meeting the next day to see if they needed more supplies, but the sedan got a flat tire and had to be repaired. Alister was calm and collected as we walked through the cold government building. I stared at him in awe as I nervously smoothed my skirt, feeling positive I was about to be reprimanded for being late.

Chapter 8

∞

The dusty old men rose from their chairs as Alister breezed through the door. I quickly moved from behind his tall frame to take the seat at his side. Reynolds gave me a smug grin as he sat down across the table from me. The anxiety I felt turned to disgust and I raised my chin defiantly.

Near the window at the back of the room, a strange woman turned to face us. Her matted dreadlocks with gold medallions dangling from the ends contrasted sharply with the burgundy business suit she wore. Around her neck was a large gold star pendent. I stared at her transfixed as she stared back at me, our eyes locked in an oddly personal embrace.

"Who is this?" Alister asked, snapping me out of the daze.

"Medea," she said softly and yet her voice filled the room. "I was in the service of your aunt before her untimely passage. My travels have kept me away for some time. I've just returned this morning. I would have been late, but as luck would have it, it seems I am right on time. I am sorry to hear about your car troubles." Something about the way she smiled unnerved me.

"I've heard your name before," Alister said. "Though I'm not sure what service you performed."

"Leave that to us," Reynolds interrupted. "It's an old matter of the previous administration we are working on. Just tying up loose ends."

"And why shouldn't I be informed about the actions of this board?" Alister narrowed his eyes.

"In good time, you will be Mr. President." Reynolds cowered under the gaze. "Once we have all the facts to present. However, we've asked Medea here today for another purpose. Due to the scene at Dives the other night and the notes from Professor Berlin, we thought it best to get Medea's opinion on Miss Vita."

My shoulders slumped as I sat back in my chair. *Why didn't I realize the professor was giving them reports?* It made sense, but I suddenly felt my trust was violated.

"Why wasn't I informed about this decision?" Alister growled.

"It is harmless. I assure you," Reynolds said. "She is just here to observe and tell us what she sees."

"What do you see?" I asked quietly, turning my attention to the exotic woman once more.

"A miracle," she smiled. "Your aura is a perfect rainbow, like the first children of the earth. It has been many years since I've seen anything like it."

"Does this make her dangerous?" the man next to Reynolds asked.

"Not in the way you think it does." Medea's eyes never left my face. "But more so than you can even imagine."

"What does this mean?" Reynolds asked. Beads of sweat gathered on his forehead.

"It means don't mess with me," I smirked, and Medea burst into laughter. The men sat frozen with looks of terror etched across their faces.

"I congratulate you on your find Mr. President," Medea said after catching her breath. "And to you Fawn. It's not often we connect with our soulmates during this lifetime."

"I refuse to see the humor in this," Reynolds said as he wiped the moisture from his face with a handkerchief. "Is Miss Vita a danger to the world? Is there something we should be aware of?"

Medea smiled contritely at the old man. "She is not a danger to the people and worrying will get you nowhere. I suggest you relax."

"You speak in riddles witch." Reynolds' tone grew bolder upon hearing the insult. "Tell us what the future holds."

The air in the room suddenly pulsed with a cold wind current. I flinched as I sat back in my chair.

"You'd do well to remember who it is that you address," Medea spoke, but I swear her lips didn't move. "I have told you what you need to know. Press me no more on this matter now. I am weary from my travels." Reynolds began to stutter and Alister raised a silencing hand.

"You disrespect your superiors," he said sternly. "And you are rude to our honored guest."

Something about the way Alister spoke caused me to eye him warily. He was present but his eyes seemed distant like he was somewhere else. I didn't understand until the room suddenly slowed around me.

The light from the dirty window grew brighter and the dust in the air stilled. Medea's face was the only thing in focus and her deep brown eyes bore into my soul. I felt warm and oddly at peace with the situation, until I realized it was super freaking weird.

"Don't worry sweet child." Her voice had the hint of laughter that pulled me in. "I've only quieted them so I can speak."

I bit my lip as I listened, not wanting to also be silenced.

"They may be monkeys, but they are dangerous. You don't belong in this mix. I can feel it in my bones. I am tired now, but I'd like to speak to you again sometime. Would this be okay?"

I slowly nodded, unsure if any other answer would suffice.

"Good," she smiled. "I need some time to reflect and so do you. Is this kind spirit orb that follows you someone you can trust?"

I shrugged. "The only spirit I know is Vorie, but I don't know what an orb is."

"Vorie," she said her name gently. "Yes. That feels right. Do you trust her?"

"With my life," I whispered.

"That's good," Medea sighed. "At least you are looked after for now, but I worry that won't be enough when the time comes."

"When what time comes?" I ventured to ask. Medea's eyelids were heavy.

"I need to seek clarity," she said. "I'll meet you again when you discover where you are."

"But I know where I am now." I looked around the room in confusion, wondering if we'd left. My vision focused. Medea was gone and the board members were talking.

"Where'd she go?" I whispered breathlessly to Alister.

"The witch?" he asked quietly. "She left a while ago. Did she speak to you too?" I nodded. "We'll talk about it later."

"This feed the portal jumpers initiative you've suggested needs serious consideration from the board. We'll give it an in-depth discussion before any measures can be taken. Six months' time should be enough to discuss and readdress," Reynolds' voice droned.

I rolled my eyes. "But we're already feeding…"

Alister laid his hand on top of my thigh and the comforting current caught me off guard. "What Miss Vita means to say is that the people are already feeding the jumpers. It would be good to take some of the burden from them." The man at the typewriter looked at his page.

"I see," he said in a nasally tone. "And we thank them for their generosity, but there are numbers to check and liabilities to account for before an endeavor of this magnitude can take place."

"But it's just food," I groaned. Alister's eyes were pleading as he looked to me.

"That may be the case." Reynolds' lips twitched into a smile as he watched mine and Alister's interaction. I instantly put my tongue in my cheek as I vowed to myself to stay quiet.

"But there are many issues at play here and careful consideration of the board is the only way to address these matters." Reynolds' eyes traveled to Alister's face. "And as for the shipment of fuel you've requested be delivered to the ghetto Mr. President, I'm afraid we had to confiscate it."

"That was not within your right," Alister glared. "How dare you overstep me."

"No disrespect." Reynolds bowed his head. "But matters of finance and distribution are the duty of this board. We will study the impact and revisit this at next month's meeting."

*

"Are you alright?" I asked Alister as I placed my hand in his. He leaned against the board room door with his jaw clenched and eyes blazing with fury.

"Yes," he sighed loudly. "I just need to work on a few things. Would you mind if the driver took you home? I'll be here for a while."

"Sure." I stood on my tiptoes to kiss his cheek. "I want to check out our illegal feeding operation anyway." He reluctantly released my hand as I headed down the hall.

Like a rat, Reynolds went scurrying quickly by me.

"Hey," I called out, freezing him in his tracks. "What were you doing with that Kingston mafia guy the other night at Dives?"

"He is an old acquaintance." Reynolds cast his beady eyes around the hall as he sulked toward an open door. He seemed more coward like without the table between us. "Why do you want to know?"

"No reason," I smirked.

*

The bags at the portals were gone. Not just one or two, all of them were gone. The people Alister paid to help said government officials confiscated them. My stomach churned at the realization that the board already knew what we did and deliberately sabotaged it. I thought about going to see Alister right away, but figured he needed time to process the meeting before I put this on his plate.

I went home instead and aggressively began to rake the leaves in the courtyard. Professor Berlin was out for the evening, so I begged Freida to let me eat in the kitchen with her. The dining room was too cold and quiet. Angrily fuming at the grand table alone didn't sound like much fun at all.

Freida left early. Odan was coming to visit for the holiday break and she wanted to get her place ready. The silence of the empty stone house was deafening, so I went to my room and blasted the music through the earbuds trying very hard not to cry.

*

"Get up," Vorie whispered in my ear.

"What time is it?" I groaned.

"Morning," she laughed. "Come take a look."

I untangled myself from the blankets and instantly regretted it. The cold slap of air froze my bare shoulders causing me to shiver uncontrollably. The warmth from the fireplace was weak. I raced over to stoke the coals and brought it roaring back to life.

"Hurry," Vorie urged me.

"Give me a second," I said through chattering teeth. "It's freezing in here."

"Get your blanket and come here," she sighed in frustration as she floated over to the window. I yanked the comforter off the bed.

"Alright. What is it?" I asked as I waddled over to her.

"Look." She pointed outside. I pressed my face against the frosted glass. Fat white puffs drifted from the sky and blanketed the street below us.

"Is this snow?" I gasped.

"It sure is," she smiled. We stared in awe as the snow piled higher on the ground.

"Is it snowing at Genie's?" I asked.

"Yep. But I'll wait to wake her up, so she doesn't chew my ear off."

"I'm glad you are here to see it with me."

"Where else would I be?"

"I don't know. With Brayson I'd assume. How is he doing by the way?"

"It's still early in the morning for him so he's probably still asleep."

"That's not what I meant. How is he doing? How are things between the two of you?"

"Difficult," she sighed. "He wants to spend all his free time with me, and I don't want him married to a ghost. He's been talking about getting another tracker. I just want him to live his life normally. Maybe meet someone who is still alive…" her voice trailed off.

"Absolutely not." I turned to face her. "Not that he'd actually do it, but could you imagine the nightmare that would be in the realm? Is he supposed to have multiple wives for all eternity?"

"It's different than you think," she laughed. "Existence is more fluid there. It's like your soul can be divided to be in many places at once."

"Is that like the orb thing?"

"Huh?" Vorie's forehead scrunched.

"I met this witch yesterday. Or at least I think that's what she is. The spirit orb that follows me, is that you?"

"Oh Medea," Vorie nodded. "Yeah, I've seen her coming. She wants to talk with me sometime. But yes, the orb is a piece of me. The piece that wants to make sure you're okay."

"Wait. You saw her coming? What else have you seen?"

Vorie put a finger over her smiling lips as he eyes grew distant.

"You better not disappear again," I warned her. "Or I'll... I don't know what I'll do, but it'll be something."

"I'm not going just yet," she laughed. "But there are some things I can't tell you until you figure them out for yourself."

"Well why the hell not?"

"Because the slightest change in your predestined path may alter your fate and I wouldn't want that," she shrugged. "Plus, you're stubborn and you need to learn things the hard way."

"Try me." I narrowed my eyes. She shook her head. "Fine then. Be mysterious. But what is this fate or destiny thing? I don't feel like I'm doing much of anything at all. I tried to make changes, tried to help people, and that group of crusty old men is blocking everything I'm trying to do."

"Just keep being you," she smiled. "You're heading down the right path."

"But what path is it?" I pulled the blanket tighter around me as I turned to watch the snow fall. "Is my path here or somewhere else? How do I even know what to do here?"

"Stay true to who you are, and you won't go wrong."

"Did you read that in a book?" I rolled my eyes.

"Sure did," she whispered. "But it's an honest truth. Now let your path take you outside to play in the snow, because I know that's where you want to be right now." When I looked away from the window she was gone.

I pulled on my boots from the wardrobe but realized I didn't have a warm enough coat. Keeping the blanket wrapped around me, I rushed down the staircase and threw open the giant arched doors.

The guards in the vehicle sat up suddenly, alerted by the movement of me coming outside. Thick white steam puffed from the exhaust pipe. The man in the passenger seat cracked open the door.

"What's going on Miss Vita?" he asked as his foot touched the curb.

"It's snowing," I laughed as he looked at me curiously. "Stay in there," I commanded, regaining my composure. "I just want to enjoy this alone right now." The guard nodded as he closed the door and cranked up the heater.

The snow was falling heavily around me, but the columned porch withstood most of the drift. I placed a tentative foot on the steps and slipped, falling unceremoniously onto my backside. The wet snow immediately soaked through my thin pants and I jumped up shrieking.

I could see the guards chuckling, but I didn't mind. It was too beautiful outside. I crunched my way down the sidewalk, leaving impressions with my boots.

"What are you doing, you crazy girl?" Freida's voice was sharp and it startled me.

"Just playing," I grinned sheepishly.

"Well get inside before you catch your death from the cold." She shivered as she hurried into the professor's house.

"I'll be right in," I called after her.

The thick grey clouds blocked out the sun, but the air was getting warmer as the morning became more alert. The guards watched me with a humorous fascination. I reached into a bank of snow and balled some between my bright red stinging hands. Then I threw it at their windshield making them both laugh harder.

The snowflakes fell lighter and I was worried they would stop soon. My blanket was soaked, but I wasn't ready to give this up yet. I walked further down the sidewalk, away from the prying eyes of the guards, and stood still letting the snow fall around me. I tilted my face to the sky and stuck out my tongue, trying to catch one of the snowflakes before they all disappeared.

"What are you doing, little deer?" Alister's voice sent warmth through the chill of the morning.

"Living." I smiled as he wrapped his arms around me.

"Let's get you inside. You're freezing."

"Just a second," I grinned. "I think I dropped something." I reached down to the ground beside me and hastily scooped up a fresh batch of snow. Then I turned around slowly and batted my eyelashes as he looked romantically into my eyes. In an instant, his hair was covered in snow and I ran laughing into the house as he chased me.

*

"I wanted to surprise you before you got up." Alister helped me hang the comforter over the rack by the fireplace.

"I'm sorry," I giggled. "But you can't compete with the surprise of seeing snow for the first time."

"Apparently not." He sat brooding as he watched me remove my wet clothes. "It seems I can't compete with anyone anymore, but I do wish I could make you as happy as the weather does."

"You make me happy." I pulled a hoodie over my head. "What is it you feel you can't compete with?" He groaned as I pulled on dry pants and turned to stare at the fire.

"The board," he sighed. "I'm not allowed to authorize a gas shipment this winter. I sent a few gallons from my personal estate to Freida to make good on my promise. She should have received it last night, but I won't be able to sneak more into the ghetto without them confiscating it in the interest of national security."

"They took the bags from the portals too." I crossed my arms. "Why are they doing this to us?"

"It's policy. They aren't used to sweeping changes and things move slowly when they do come."

"The people need food now. They don't have time to wait. There are less of them every day. Can't you just overrule the board or something?"

"That isn't how it works." He shook his head. "I don't know how Marley got them to do her bidding. I'm learning I have less control than I thought."

Probably because she was an evil bitch, I thought. "Okay, what can we do?"

"Play the game," he shrugged. "And move the chess pieces in our favor when the opportunity presents itself. Speaking of that, there are some winter events we will be required to attend soon."

"Is this truly winter?" I looked out the window. The snow had stopped falling.

"Not yet," he said. "It's just an early storm. It'll get a lot worse as the season continues."

"This isn't so bad now," I smiled. "But maybe we should hurry to help the people before it does get worse."

Alister sighed. "I'm studying ways to work around the protocol, but it'll take more time."

I walked across the room and put my arms over his shoulders. "I'll help you find a way."

"You can help me in another way." His eyes shone with mischief.

"Not now." I grabbed his hand and pulled him down the hall. "Freida will be angry if we are late for breakfast."

Chapter 9

∞

The castle drawbridge sat at the portal exit, waiting ominously for us to cross it. Eight guards dressed in black stood silently flanking me and Alister as we prepared to enter.

"Is there a reason I couldn't pick my own glamour?" I looked down at the ruffled white sleeves that flared at my wrist and the tight black corset which ended in a cage skirt. Yards of fabric lined the cage swaying delicately as I turned. I was grateful it was only glamour because I wouldn't have been able to walk if I had to actually carry all the weight of the outfit.

"PR usually decides what we wear to these events," Alister smiled. He looked handsome in his black tailcoat and pantaloons.

"I don't have antlers, do I?" I tried unsuccessfully to look at the top of my head.

"No," he laughed. "Should I put in a special request for next time?"

"Let's just get this over with," I said, rolling my eyes. I placed one booted foot on the bridge and the guards followed. I wasn't sure what to expect at this celebration feast, but my one consolation was that Genie would be there.

As we walked down the torch lit stone hallway, I repeated the advice I was given like a mantra. *Sit still. Smile big. Nod when appropriate. Try not to disagree with anyone...* I'd give the agreement thing my best shot for just this one night.

The grand feast was a yearly event where the highest elites and world leaders all gathered for the evening to celebrate. When I'd asked what it was we were celebrating, I was told it was a tradition based off the old American Thanksgiving holiday. Breaking bread with different countries and keeping the mutual respect alive. When I didn't receive an answer as to why only the rich attended, I realized exactly what it was they were celebrating.

I raised my chin as I entered the dining hall. *It's just one night. How bad can it be?*

Inside the open room, there was no ceiling. We were in an open courtyard with stone watch towers pointing toward a vibrant starry night. I stared at the sky in awe, wishing it was real.

As we continued forward, my eyes traveled over the rows of bench tables with silver platters piled high with various foods. I instantly spotted Genie in her bright red gown sitting squished between her in-laws and Craton. She stood when she saw me, and we waved to each other before her mother-in-law pulled her back down by her elbow.

"We're over here," Alister nodded to the table directly across from Genie's.

"We can't sit with her?" I asked as I motioned to my friend.

"It's assigned seating," he shrugged. I pouted my lip in Genie's direction and smiled when she did the same. Alister escorted me to our places.

The cornucopia of food in front of me sure looked appetizing. A husky man directly across from us dipped a glistening roll into a pot of steaming gravy while gnawing on a turkey leg. My stomach growled, but I knew none of these illusions would sedate my hunger.

"Just pretend," Alister whispered in my ear. I watched him fill his plate, and then shook my head as he chewed thoughtfully on an ear of corn.

"How do you do it?" I whispered back. "Doesn't it feel so stupid?"

"Just eat little deer," he winked. "I promise I'll get you some real food on the way home." Sighing, I put some potatoes on my plate and dressed them with butter.

The next hour was a gluttonous feast. The food never ran out and the wine jugs never emptied, even as I watched the greedy hands of the diners around me constantly reaching for more. As their voices grew louder, I lost myself while watching the shooting stars in the manifested night sky.

"I, for one, think it's fantastic. Such an edgy and progressive move from this handsome new president. Don't you agree?" The woman sitting next to me tapped my arm.

"Excuse me?" I asked, shaking off the dreamy daze.

"She was wondering if you think it is modern and inventive to appoint an orphan as his running mate," the husky man explained while using his fingernail to pick his teeth. Alister's face was neutral, but I saw the hint of anger flash in his eyes.

"So modern." I turned to the woman smiling. "He is a very progressive and enlightened president."

"Aren't you just the luckiest rags to riches story ever?" the woman giggled as she swayed in her seat.

"So lucky," I said sweetly through clinched teeth. "It's like a dream come true."

"She is the most darling little thing," the woman crooned as she leaned behind me to rub her hand down Alister's arm. "Wherever did you find her?"

"If you'll excuse us," Alister said calmly as he stood from the bench. "The music is about to begin, and I'd like to ask Miss Vita to dance."

"What was that all about?" I asked once we were out of earshot.

"Preconceived notions and ignorant people." He held out his hand as the orchestra started. "Don't worry about them."

We moved slowly in step with the vibrating notes. Genie and Craton sided up next to us.

"This place sucks," Genie moaned, causing me to chuckle. "Can't we just get out of here?" I gave Alister pleading eyes.

"Typically, we wait for the guest speaker," he said.

"Are we going to miss something important if we don't stay?" I smiled mischievously.

"Not anything they haven't already said every other year," Craton grinned.

"I guess if you're not feeling well Miss Vita, it would be improper of me to not escort you home." Alister looked lovingly at me, causing my heart to swell.

"I do need to eat something," I laughed. "I really don't feel well." Genie suddenly growled beside me. I turned to see what she was glaring at.

In the corner of one of the bench tables, Kingston sat with a group of mafia thugs. His bulging eyes were staring straight at me and a grotesque smile played on his face. I shivered and stepped closer to Genie.

How did I not see him there? Then again, how had I not seen him in the shadows my whole life… This isn't fair. What did I do to draw this jerk's attention? I felt instantly sweaty and shut my eyes. *Just go away! I want you to disappear…*

"Stop little deer," Alister commanded in my ear. The gasps and squeals of the diners cleared my head. When I opened my eyes, I saw all the food from the tables was gone and the décor was slightly askew.

"Put it back if you can," Alister whispered. "Hurry."

I blinked and everything returned to normal, minus the confusion on everyone's faces.

"What just happened?" Genie was clinging to my arm.

"Glitch in the system?" I shrugged guiltily.

"Must have been a glitch," Alister nodded. "Let's get out of here."

"Are you leaving so soon, President Macavay?" Reynolds asked as we walked past him and two other board members.

"This glitch shows that the manifestation is unstable," Alister said coldly. "Perhaps you should think about leaving too."

The other attendees heard Alister's words and nervously began to rise. An anxious commotion spread throughout the room.

Reynolds narrowed his eyes at me. "There has never been a glitch before as long as Kingston has been checking the system. Don't you find this strange Miss Vita?" Hearing the monster's name spoken so casually caused bile to rise in my throat.

"Not really," I struggled to keep the disgust from my voice. "The older one gets, the easier it is to make mistakes."

The crowd was growing more restless as people began to leave. Genie and Craton joined our huddle as the government guards directed us to the drawbridge. All the while, a plan was formulating in my head to destroy the monster's life.

*

Genie and I sat on the edge of the broken overpass while Craton and Alister talked on the hoods of the cars below. The guards were taking shifts sleeping in their vehicles, casting angry glances our way intermittently. We'd purchased some of Porter's brew and driven to a meeting point in the countryside. It'd been a long night of drinking and laughing. Now the dawn was threatening to break on the horizon.

"Hear me out." I swung my legs over the concrete ledge and Genie rested back on her arms. "What if I start to mess with places in the realm, specifically the ones that Kingston guy is supposed to inspect? I could destroy his reputation and end his career."

"As much as I want to see him burn, Vorie doesn't want us to do anything," Genie sighed.

"But I have to do something." I threw a broken piece of asphalt into the ravine below. "I'm tired of just sitting here. The stupid board is stopping all our plans to help the people. I feel like I can't ever leave the professor's house. They won't even let me have a phone. I just keep getting paraded around like a doll. It feels like I'm trapped. I need to do something to set myself free and change this world for the better. It's such a miserable existence and I hate that I'm not doing anything to stop it."

Genie leaned forward to look at Craton and Alister below us. "You know we couldn't have asked for better lives than the ones we have now. We're orphans, Fawn. Just nobodies and look how far we've come. I'm married to one of the richest men in the country and he loves me. Not only does the president love you, but you're like the freaking vice president now. We shouldn't do anything to mess this up," she cautioned.

I watched as the clouds turned a lighter gray. The sun would crest the ridge at any moment. "It's because we are orphans that we should fight back. No one will ever care for us like we do."

Genie silently watched the sky dissolve. The morning rays finally broke through and illuminated her golden hair. "I don't have a phone either," she nodded. "Alright. Let me speak with Fergus to see if he can get a list of places Kingston inspects."

"Fergus?" I swallowed hard.

Genie rolled her eyes. "He'd still do anything for you. Why do you think he requested to work for Craton's father?"

*

"Are you ready yet?" Alister stood outside my open bedroom door.

"I feel like a stuffed teddy bear," I called back as I tried to zip the down feather parka. "How do people wear these many layers?" I sucked in my stomach as tightly as I could and finally managed to get the zipper up.

"You dress for the weather," Alister chuckled. "It's cold outside. I want you to be warm."

"These boots aren't very comfortable," I groaned as I waddled over to him. "And my arms can't go flat against my side." I raised my arms up and down to prove my point.

"It still amazes me that you've never experienced a real winter." He put his arm around my waist.

"It amazes me that anyone can breathe with all this gear." I tugged at the scarf around my neck and adjusted the beanie.

"You look beautiful," he smiled. "And trust me, you'll be glad you are wearing this."

*

The frost nipped at my nose as we stood on the main street of the ghetto. This was the last stop for the night. We'd been driving around for hours, visiting various areas in the vicinity to hand out what the government called "winter gifts."

"This doesn't look the same," I whispered to Alister as we looked out over the crowd. There were no fire barrels, no laughter. The street was swept clean and the people stood shivering in their Sunday best as they listened to the announcer speak of prosperity and gratitude.

"I think it's just the formality of it all," he spoke softly into my ear. "They are trying to make a good impression."

I watched a little girl with blue tinted lips cling tightly to her mother's skirt. She was trying to be silent, but I could see the cold and length of the speech were bothering her. The mother laid a comforting hand on her head but shushed her all the same.

"Shouldn't we be the ones trying to make a good impression on the people?" I asked him.

"We are." He arched an eyebrow. "The board has us dressed up and paraded to all these events in order to give a good impression of the government. It's mostly just for show. Plus, we are bringing them extra food for the winter."

"But look, they are scared." I directed his attention to the girl I'd been watching. "They don't want to be out here. The kids are cold. It's like they are doing this because they are forced to show respect."

"That's just the way things are," he shrugged. "People respect us because we take care of them."

My thoughts turned to the town meeting in the village. *Everyone warm and comfortable enough to speak their minds…*

"They don't respect you. They fear you." My brain raced as I tried to rationalize it all. "We work for them, right? There are elections. That means people hire you to do a job."

"In a sense, yes." Alister nodded.

"Then why are they standing out here freezing in the street while we are up on this stage?"

"It's the way it's always been…"

*

"Why do you look so distraught?" Alister pulled me closer to him in the back seat of the sedan.

"I don't feel like what we are doing is right." I stared at the floor mat beneath my feet.

"But we gave them extra food for the winter. A gift from the National Reserves. I thought this would make you happy."

I remembered the boxes of food Brayson and I had brought with us to the wild. "We didn't give them nearly enough." I shook my head. "Why couldn't we give them more?"

"Because then we'd run out," Alister said. "And we need that for a real emergency. What's gotten into you Fawn? I know you are smarter than this. We can't support everyone, then people wouldn't support themselves."

"I know," I sighed as I looked out the window. The winterized city flew by. "It's just the looks on their faces, the silent complicity despite the hardness of their circumstances. It was hard to see. Why don't they fight it? The government wouldn't exist without them. They are the ones who vote, who work. They pay with their labor and their produce. Why don't they change the rules themselves, so they don't have to suffer?"

"Well then we'd be out of a job," Alister chuckled.

"Maybe it'd be for the better."

*

"I know what you're doing, and I don't like it." Vorie folded her ghostly arms over her chest.

"Just tell me what Genie said," I begged.

"I told you to leave it alone. What he did was wrong, but I don't want your blood on my hands." She paced around the bedroom. Her feet never touched the floor.

"Your blood is on my hands though, Vorie." I sighed as I fell back onto the bed. "I couldn't stop what happened, but now I can help right the wrong. Just please tell me what she said."

"No." Vorie shook her head. "I don't need you to avenge me. This isn't part of your destiny."

"I don't care about my stupid destiny." I put my hands over my face and groaned. "I literally can't do anything. The stupid board blocks my every move and treats every idea I have with cold disdain. If I don't do something to change the status quo, I'm going to explode."

Vorie stood unnaturally still. I peeked through my fingers to see her eyes glazed over as she stared above my head. Her spirit form began to convulse.

"What's happening?" I shrieked. "Are you okay?"

"What's wrong?" She blinked and looked momentarily confused as she glanced around the room.

"What was that seizure thing you just did? You scared the crap out of me."

"Nothing," she said as she came to sit next to me. "If you do this, things are going to accelerate much faster than intended."

I eyed her with concern, worried she'd do that weird thing again. "I have to do something," I said softly, not wanting to upset her. "I can't just sit here. Please tell me what Genie said."

Vorie's eyes filled with translucent tears. "Fine," she nodded. "There is a new zoo, the one that Brayson wanted to design. The grand opening is tomorrow. She'll meet you at the gate at nine."

"I promise this is for the best," I called out as her spirit drifted away.

Chapter 10

∞

"Um. Why is he here?" I stood leaning against the hallway wall in the realm as Genie entered through the portal with Fergus. I honestly didn't mean to be rude. It was just a shock seeing him so close after all this time.

"Craton couldn't come, and he insisted I bring a bodyguard." Genie rolled her eyes. "Plus, he did hack the system to find a list of the places Kingston has signed off on."

"You know I can hear you right?" Fergus cocked his head to the side. The dimple on his cheek deepened as he smiled.

"Speaking of guards..." Genie breezed past us as she went to inspect the glamour windows. "Where are yours Miss Vita?"

I blushed as I looked to my feet. "I might have climbed over the courtyard back wall." Genie started laughing.

"Did you not want me to be here?" Fergus asked gently.

"It's not that," I sighed as I raised my face to meet his eyes. "It's just kind of awkward with how things happened at the club."

"Fair enough," he nodded. "Why don't we start over? I'd still like to be your friend." He reached out his hand to shake mine. "My name is Fergus. I work for the mafia. I run maintenance on people to make sure they are doing what they're supposed to. I'm also a destroyer. It's nice to meet you."

I smiled in spite of myself. "It's nice to meet you too," I said as I gripped his hand.

"Are we friends yet?" Genie yelled from the end of the hall. Fergus and I nodded.

"Perfect." She clapped her hands. "Now let's talk about disguises."

"How about you don't disguise anything and just go back to your own home? Heck, you can even come to mine." Vorie materialized in the hall. Genie and I jumped into each other's arms squealing at her sudden appearance.

"What the hell Vorie? You scared the shit out of me." Genie pulled her fingernails off my wrist.

"Maybe you should be scared." Vorie crossed her arms. "You're playing a dangerous game."

I sighed as I walked over to give her a real hug. "I have to do this." Genie wrapped her arms around us both.

Vorie rested her chin on the top of Genie's head as she stared into my eyes. "Are you ready to face the consequences of this?"

114

"I am. No matter what they may be."

"One day, I want you to not have to learn things the hard way." Vorie stepped back from our embrace. "Go then, before I find a way to stop you." Genie and I locked arms as we motioned for Fergus to hurry up and join us.

"Fergus," Vorie said coldly as he passed.

"It's nice to see you again," he mumbled as we grabbed his arms and manifested to the Peregrinuz Zoo of Wonders.

*

Daylight in the realm always weirds me out. Stepping from the grayish nothing into a sudden blast of light is a little nauseating. Recalling the professor's lesson, I almost manifested a pair of sunglasses, but Genie would have a heart attack if she knew I could create glamour. Better to stick to the mission and the blinding light.

We passed the crowd of tourists waiting for their tickets in the line. Our trackers were already loaded with the entrance code. *I guess it pays to be elite.*

The trees and plants inside rose statue like from the ground. Unnatural colors in neon shades took the greens and browns by surprise. The resulting effect was a distorted and whimsical interpretation of what a real jungle should look like. It was overwhelming and I had to fight the urge to make it go away.

A young boy who was maybe ten stood on a rock handing out maps. My heart ached as I took one from him and he gave me the same cordial smile I'd used all my life for the paying customers.

Without thinking, I leaned forward to whisper in his ear, "We are orphans too."

He turned to size Genie and me up, taking in our outfits and appearance. I was hoping my words would connect with him, give him motivation for the future. Instead, he dropped his head humbly so as not to appear rude.

"Maybe you once were, ma'am," he whispered before turning to hand a map to the next customers in line. His sweet little voice, and the fear in his eyes, fueled the pent-up anger inside me. The professor's words played in my mind. *Feel it, but let it pass.*

"Where exactly are we going?" Fergus studied the map over my shoulders.

"I'll know it when I see it." I hastily folded the map and stormed down the path before us.

To our right was a unicorn enclosure. Graceful equine beings stood on a grassy knoll and sipped water from a deep blue lake. The mist rising from the water added to the magical effect. Their milky white skin, golden horns, and dark purple eyes were perfect manifestations of a fairy tale.

Suddenly, a Pegasus flew in with his silver wings and the unicorns went galloping up the hill. The muscles in his powerful legs rippled as he kneeled to the water's edge and he drank deeply from the lake. I pulled myself away from the scene. They wouldn't be able to help.

"How about the dragon?" Genie whispered as we passed the giant cage. The beast's kind eyes turned tiredly toward me as he curled up next to a boulder.

"Too lazy," I shook my head.

"If we are looking for the most dangerous ones," Fergus leaned down to speak in my ear. "The dinosaurs are at the end of the park down there." He pointed to a walkway lined by black and white trees with puffs of pink cotton swaying in the manifested breeze.

"Too far from the entrance." I continued walking down the main path. A few steps later, I found what I needed.

The crowds had gathered at the main exhibit and their cruel cheers egged on the snarling animals behind the predator cages. Wolves, lions, bears, and crocodiles all snapped at the bars that held them back from the taunting tourists.

"This will work," I smiled brightly.

Genie shivered beside me. "I know no one can get hurt, but this still seems kind of dangerous."

"Well let's get out of here then." I pulled her arm through mine and we turned to walk back to the entrance.

Fergus looked over his shoulder as he raced to catch up with us. "What's the plan? What do we need to do?"

"I just needed to see it." I closed my eyes as we walked, imagining just the cages. I wanted them to fall. I wanted the animals to be set free.

The blood curdling screams from the crowd behind us assured me it had worked. Genie and Fergus spun around to look at the chaos, but I didn't need to see that.

The manifested animals were rushing forward, hell bent on extracting retribution from their tormentors. With no gates between them, the people were suddenly thrust into panic, forgetting they couldn't be hurt as they clamored over one another in their attempt to get away.

"Are you going to put them back?" Genie gasped as she clung to me. "I don't want to get trampled when the crowd comes this way."

"Just a minute." I continued to walk toward the boy with the maps. His mouth hung open and his eyes were wide as he stood looking at the disaster behind us. I released Genie's hand and leaned downed to his face.

His confusion turned to fear as he met my eyes once more. I smiled my warmest smile as I snapped my fingers in the air. The gates instantly returned. The boy's head was on a swivel as he looked to the restored cages and back to me.

"I'm still an orphan," I said.

A smiled teased his lips. "Yeah. I can see it now."

*

"Can I speak with you a second?" Fergus asked before I reached the portal.

"Sure," I said as I looked to Genie. She was anxiously waiting by the panel.

"Hurry up," she urged us. "I want to get out of here."

"I'm sorry about what happened at The Nocere and I'm sorry for how things turned out between us." He stared at me with tormented eyes.

"It's okay." I placed my hand comfortingly on his arm. "But there is no us. I need you to understand that." I thought of Alister working in his office late into the night, trying to help the people, and I instantly felt horrible for even being in this position.

119

"We can still be friends, as long as you promise not to always try to protect me," I laughed.

Fergus chuckled softly. "Friends is fine. I'd hate to lose you again. And I'll try not to be so protective, but I would like to help. Is there anything I can do?"

"Why do you want to help me so badly?" I asked.

"I told you this already. There is something about you, something good. Even your destruction is not like mine. It's calmer and comes from kindness if that makes sense. Maybe I'm a little jealous, or maybe I just want to learn. Either way, I feel like it's my duty to help you."

"Okay," I smiled. "Do you think you can find out more about this Kingston guy? I mean, I know we know he is higher up in the mafia and works with the portal technology, but I'd like to know where he lives and where he goes. It'd be nice to have the upper hand because I'm sure if I keep threatening his work, he'll find a way to come for me again."

*

I should have been able to gracefully climb the courtyard wall, but the ice-covered ivy vine broke under my weight. The crashing sound of my back hitting the sidewalk brought the night watch guards running over to investigate with their pistols drawn.

"It's just me guys." I raised my hands under the beam of their flashlights and moaned as I sat up from the ground.

"I was just testing to see if I could sneak out," I giggled nervously. "Apparently I cannot." They helped me to my feet and shook their heads as they guided me through the front door of the professor's house.

*

"Was it worth it?" Vorie sat on the edge of my bed as I pulled my aching body onto it.

"It was," I nodded. "He needs to be punished for what he did, but we couldn't punish him ourselves. If I keep this up, then he will get in trouble by someone else. We are just helping karma along." I closed my eyes as my head hit the pillow.

"It was kind of neat to see them all freak out," she sighed. I smiled as I drifted off to sleep.

*

"Look at this handsome escort." I rushed down the steps toward Alister who stood waiting by the open door of the sedan. He gave me a confused smile. After he'd shut the door behind us, I wrapped my arms around his shoulders and planted my lips on top of his.

121

"You're in a good mood," he said dreamily once I finally pulled my lips away. "What caused this?"

"I feel like I'm actually getting something accomplished," I laughed.

"Care to tell me what that is?" He leaned back against the seat, the happy grin still plastered across his face.

"All in good time. I want to see if the plan actually works first." I laced his fingers through my fingers and moved his arm up so I could snuggle against his chest. "Do you have time to spend with me after the board meeting today? I want you all to myself."

"I think I can move some stuff around," he sighed in content as he rested his chin on top of my head. "I'd do anything for you, little deer."

*

"What do you mean you won't feed them?" The bitterness of frustration and anger built up the sound of my voice. "It's just extra food to you, but it will keep them healthy and you won't have to lose anymore citizens than you already have."

"We've decided that it isn't in our best interest to waste supplies on those who are not willing to help themselves," the old man at the end of the table glanced nervously at his notes as he spoke.

122

"And what about the extra gas for the winter? The citizens that live in the ghetto work. Can you not help them?" I could feel my blood beginning to boil.

"We've decided to shelve that discussion for the time being and reevaluate it in the spring."

"But they are cold now!" I slammed my palm against the table.

Alister placed a calming hand on top of mine. "If the gas comes from my personal estate, I order you to not detain another shipment."

"Unfortunately, Mr. President, in your position, any donations made from your property must be passed by the vote of this board," Reynolds said.

"What are we even here for?" I scanned the faces of the men. "Are we just puppets in your control?"

"There is more to it than that," Reynolds reassured me with a malicious humor in his eyes. "You two are the face of the government and you must be protected at all costs. Speaking of which, it seems that you were witnessed leaving the scene of another unfortunate glitch last night in the realm at Peregrinuz Zoo of Wonders. Where were your guards?" I felt the muscles in Alister's hand stiffen.

"I don't know what you are talking about," I glared at him.

"Oh, but I think you do," he smirked. "The night shift mentioned that you had an accident on the courtyard wall last night practicing your escape. Very odd indeed. What boggles us is how coincidental it is that you were there for the last two major glitches in the realm. Don't you find this peculiar, Miss Vita?"

He reached into his briefcase as he continued speaking, "And from Professor Berlin's notes it seems that you are more than capable of causing these anomalies." He pulled out the yellow pages from the professor's notebook and I felt sick all over again. I knew he was required to report on me, but those familiar pages felt more personal than a simple report.

"You have no real proof," I smiled coldly.

"True," Reynolds shrugged. "But it is in the best interest of this board, and of our great nation, that we limit your movements for the foreseeable future and provide extra security for your protection. We've decided that visiting public places in the realm would be too dangerous for you right now."

"You've got to be kidding me!" I furiously rose from my chair. Alister and I locked eyes. His were filled with a confused outrage and mine were blinded with hate.

"I'll be in your office," I said. "Come find me when you're done with these bastards."

Chapter 11

∞

I paused as I pushed open the heavy wooden door to Alister's office. The last time I'd been in that room was the day Marley ordered a new tracker to be placed in my arm and I hadn't come back since. Fueled by the frustration of being trapped and helpless by the board, I shook off whatever trepidation I'd harbored and closed the door behind me.

The room was as big as I remembered. I eyed the circular couch and decided to sit at the grand oak desk by the windows instead. The rolling chair reclined, and I leaned against it as I watched the clouds drift by.

There has to be a way to work around them. It's just a chess game. I need to figure out the next move. Maybe we can figure out a way to get rid of them all, I smirked.

The chair squeaked as I leaned back too far. I quickly sat upright. Letting the calm resolve of forming a plan wash over me, I twirled the chair around to face the desk.

I will figure this out. It will be okay.

Alister's desk was neatly organized and I smiled to myself upon seeing it. *Maybe we weren't so different after all.* I pictured the late nights he spent learning and working here, trying to be the best president he could be, and I admired him even more.

Resting my head on top of the desk, I took a deep and steadying breath. *Maybe it's wrong of me to focus this hard on bringing down Kingston. If Vorie doesn't care, why should I?*

Because I feel responsible, I groaned to myself. *And I have the power to do something about it. It's not like I can do anything else, that stupid board is a government joke...*

"Oh, I'm sorry Miss Vita. I didn't think anyone would be in here." I looked up from the desk to see the clerk who worked down the hall with a stack of folders in his hands. "President Macavay asked for these files. I'll just leave them on the desk if you don't mind."

"Sure," I smiled at him. He didn't look much older than me, but his nervousness in my presence made me feel ancient and sad. He quickly set down the files and hurried away with his head bowed.

Did curiosity really kill the cat?

*

My jaw was clenched, and I'd tied back my hair, as I scoured the contents of the files. Blueprints and pages of symbols like the ones I'd seen on the grates at The Nocere were spread across the desk. Words in Latin and design elements in acronyms lay before me like a puzzle. The sick feeling of dread coiled in the pit of my stomach.

"I can't believe you went to the realm without any guards," Alister reprimanded me as he walked into the office. "What were you thinking?"

I looked to him wild eyed as his words bounced off me. "What is this?" I held up a page of the strange symbols.

His face blanched as he stared at the paper. "Where did you get that?"

"The clerk dropped it off a few minutes ago at your request." I shook my head in disbelief at the question I was about to ask. "Are you building another club like The Nocere?"

"I am not." He crossed the room and snatched the page from my hand. "I would never do something like that." He studied the symbols silently before letting the paper fall to the desk.

"Alister," my voice cracked with fear as he sat heavily on the chair and placed his head in his hands. "Tell me what this is."

"I didn't want to let you know until I had a solution." His green eyes glistened with tears as he turned his face to me. "This is Marley's work. Or it was her work. Now it goes deeper than anyone can imagine. They are all working on it, every country around the globe, trying to see who can enact the technology first and control it."

"What technology?" The tears in his eyes increased the panic rising within me.

"The in between." He rubbed his hand on the back of his neck. "The Nocere was just a test to see if it could work. That's why they allowed the club to be built under the financing from the patrons."

"A test for what to work?" My voice was a whisper as I asked.

"A test to see if they could control incoming spirits."

I fought to understand the meaning of it all as the fear threatened to choke me. "Why would they want to control spirits?"

"They want to control everything." He blinked his eyes dry and the steely resolve I knew so well settled across his face. "They want to control the afterlife. Whoever masters this technology first will rule eternity."

"I'm going to be sick." I clutched my hands across my stomach as the nausea washed over me. Alister moved quickly to my side and reached to caress my hair.

"Don't touch me." I glared at him. "How long have you known about this?"

He pulled back his arm and let it drop uselessly to his side. "Not that long. I knew the board was up to something. They kept talking about a cause. I finally figured it out, and then asked for the files to prove it."

"How do we stop this?" I glanced at the symbols and a new jolt of panic hit me again.

"I don't know yet," he said firmly. "I will find a way."

"If it's as big as you say it is, how will you be able to stop it?" I rose shakily from the desk chair. The heartbreak was written on his face as he looked to me, but I didn't want his pity. "Tell me what your plan is to fix this."

"I don't know, but I'll figure it out," he whispered, less convincing this time.

"I have to go." I held the desk for support as I walked around it.

"Fawn, please don't be angry with me. You know I'll do anything in my power to fix this." He caught me in his arms as I walked to the door. "I love you, little deer. Let this be my problem. I don't want you to worry about it."

I pressed my forehead against his as the tears rolled down my cheeks. "I love you too, but there is nothing you can do. You have no real power. You are nothing more than a puppet, just like I am."

My words stung him. I could feel his hurt as he stepped away. Raising my chin with the last bit of strength I could muster I turned and left the room.

*

The drive to the professor's house was a blur. I kept trying not to cry. Tears wouldn't solve anything. *Honestly nothing would.*

I remembered the faces of the elites at the feast, greedily grabbing for more imaginary food. *How can they think of something like this? Is the need for power that great?*

I tried to rationalize this situation, looking for positives. The technology still hasn't been fully built. It's just an idea right now. Maybe it will never happen.

How much time do we have until it is built though? A day, a year? They'll all want to be the first ones to make it so they can rule. And what will they rule?

I'd seen the spirits at The Nocere. They weren't whole because they didn't cross over completely. They had to know it would be a horrible existence for anyone caught in the traps.

I'm sure they do know. A tear forced its way down my face. *It'll be a separation between the ones who can afford to pay to cross over and the ones they want to rule. The orphans, the laborers, the outcasts no one wants... They won't let us crossover.*

I had to leave that logic where it was, I couldn't bear to think about what it would look like. I felt helpless and numb. *Just another cog in the turning gear leading to this eventual hell.*

At least it's only going to trap incoming spirits. *Vorie will be safe. She can live out the rest of eternity in peace. Maybe if I go now too, I won't have to deal with this anymore. I could get everyone I love to leave, and they'd all be safe...*

Regret at thinking these thoughts caused a new round of tears to fall.

*

The driver parked in front of the professor's house. I quickly dried my eyes as the guard opened the back door.

"Everything alright Miss Vita?" His face was full of concern. I nodded numbly as I walked past him, afraid that if I spoke, I would break.

The entryway was cold and dark. I stepped around the paintings enclosed in glass. They were nothing more than a pretty display of how life could have been, and I felt eerily similar to them. *Useless...*

As I neared the staircase that led to my room, I heard a loud crash coming from the kitchen. I shook away the feelings of self-pity and ran to see if Freida was okay.

*

"I'm alright," Freida groaned as I helped her to stand and guided her to a stool. "Don't fuss over me. I'm just clumsy."

I picked up the pieces of the shattered pie plate on the floor. It was her favorite blue ceramic one.

"You don't look alright," I said. Her eyes were puffy and red.

"Don't mind me," she coughed to clear the pain in her voice. "I'm just a silly old woman."

"Want to tell me what happened?" I stood up and carried the jagged shards over to the bin.

"I just slipped," she sighed.

"I can tell something is bothering you." I took the kettle from the stove and poured her a cup of tea. "You aren't getting off that easy. Tell me what is wrong."

She took a sip of her tea and began to sob. I slid a napkin into her hand and sat on the stool on the other side of the counter to wait.

"It's nothing major," she croaked after blowing her nose into the cloth. "Odan informed me that he is spending winter break in the realm. He is young and his friends will be there. I understand completely. I just miss him is all."

I reached out and clasped her hand in mine as she stared out the window. After a few moments, she shook her tired head.

"Enough of this," she said resolutely. "I have work to do."

"Do you mind if I help?" I asked gently. She patted the top of my hand.

"Of course you can sweetheart," she smiled. "Just don't cut anymore onions today."

We worked in kindred silence preparing the rack of scones for the professor's holiday party at the university the next day. I wanted to smack Odan for the pain he caused his mother, but in this I was useless too. Keeping busy helped pass the time until Professor Berlin arrived for dinner. I didn't know if speaking to him would help, but I didn't know what else to do.

*

I waited until after Freida served the food and I was sure she was out of earshot. Of all the things I wanted to do right then, causing her more worry wasn't one of them. I pushed the plate away from me and laid my arms on the table.

"Did you know what they were planning to do?"

"What who was planning to do?" Professor Berlin looked up from his book with a spoonful of succotash balanced in midair.

"In the realm, or I guess the in between. The technology they want to implement to rule the afterlife." I kept my tone even, swallowing the bitterness of the words. He placed his spoon down on his plate and removed the spectacles from his face.

"I suppose I did know." He rubbed a hand over his tired eyes. "I'm assuming Alister has taken up his aunt's plans and that's how you know."

I bit my lip as I nodded, not wanting to say anything that would stop him from telling me the truth.

"Better him than them," the professor sighed. "He would be a fair ruler. Not as cruel as some of the others."

"And you are okay with this? No objections to the idea itself?" I kept on my poker face, allowing no trace of emotion to shine through.

"It was only a matter of time before this happened," he said. "I honestly am surprised it has taken this long. Human nature, human greed, isn't satisfied without power. There is nothing left in this world. The next logical step would be to rule the other side. Do I agree? No. But I am not a power-driven man. I strive for knowledge, nothing more."

"And have you ever thought of using that knowledge to help others?" I asked softly. "Isn't your job to teach?"

"It is." He raised his eyes to the challenge. "But you can't teach unwilling students."

"Have you tried?" I met his stare with my own.

"Of course I've tried. For years I've tried. But no one wants to listen. There is nothing more that we can do besides hope for a good leader. If Alister takes that role, I have no doubt that the afterlife will remain a paradise."

"You and I both know that Alister is only a pawn for the board. They are the ones who hold the real power."

"As its always been," he sighed. "But if he acts like Marley did, he can take the ultimate power right out from under them."

My jaw tightened as I studied my reflection in the silverware, no doubt polished by Freida that morning. "And were you helping Marley? The same way you help the board by giving notes on me?"

"I do as I am told," he said. "I have no other option."

"You can fight it."

"An old man like me?"

"You can at least try."

"What good would that do?" he asked. I glared past him defiantly. My mind was already made.

A small smile turned my lips. "You say you've learned from me, but you have learned nothing at all."

"That is not true," Professor Berlin huffed in outrage. "I've been listening. I even changed the lessons at the university to include classes on practical life in your honor."

"That isn't the point anymore." I shook my head as I rose from the chair. "You had the voice to fight against this and you stayed silent. That isn't living, that's just existing. You don't know how to live so you can't teach it."

I rushed from the room with my heart pounding against my ribcage. I knew it wasn't his fault, but I was angry. Maybe angrier with myself because I almost agreed with him in my weak moment earlier that day. *Almost…*

The courtyard. The thought tugged at my mind as I neared the staircase to my room. *I need to be outside.*

"Is everything alright?" Freida called from the kitchen as I darted past the door.

"It will be once I figure it out," I paused to smile reassuringly at her.

Chapter 12

∞

I sat on the cold stone bench in the dark of the courtyard. The light from the kitchen window dimly lit the walkway but the back portion, with the barren elm and cherry blossom trees, was hauntingly shadowed.

Drawing in a calming breath, I let the events of the day unfold before me. I needed to push the feeling of hopelessness away. *There has to be a plan. I just need to figure it out...*

"Do you know where you are yet?" I heard the strangely spoken words in my head rather than with my ears. The image of her knowing eyes staring into mine came clearly in my mind.

"Medea?" I shivered.

"Here child." She walked out from behind the tree trunks and moved slowly like a cat as she came to sit beside me.

"How long have you been out here?" I placed my hand over my heart. Medea was real flesh and blood, not a ghostly apparition like Vorie, but the effect was still the same.

"I've only just arrived." The charms in her dreadlocks jingled as she swept her hair to the side, and the oversized star pendant around her neck caught a beam of light from the kitchen window. "I came to ask you if you know where you are yet."

I glanced over at the silent birdbath in confusion. *In my garden… In the courtyard I tended… At the professor's house… In Washington D.C…. These aren't the words she wants to hear.*

"In a cage," I whispered.

"Yes, you are," Medea nodded. "So, you'll understand why you need to leave. You won't be able to do anything here, not while they have you trapped."

"Can you tell me why? Why is this happening? Why am I in this position? Why me?" Fresh tears formed in my eyes. I knew she was right, I could feel it in my bones, but I needed to know more. I was sick and tired of not having all the answers.

"Sweet rainbow child." Her voice was rich and velvety, drawing me into the sound of each word. "The old ones say that the first humans on earth had your rainbow aura. A perfectly balanced and complete soul whose only purpose was to live. Many things have changed since then. Human's souls are no longer as full because they have different purposes to achieve during this life that will aid them in eternity. Your path is clear and your powers in the realm are limitless because your purpose is to live."

"That's what the professor says." I wiped my eyes with the back of my hand.

"The professor is wise in some ways and ignorant in others. As are we all. The ignorance in people breeds fear though. Alister saved you because he was afraid you'd be hurt, but there are still those who will try to use you or destroy you if you get in their way. Small minds keep you under lock and key."

"Do you know what they are doing?" I asked. "Do you know their plans for the realm?"

"Yes, I know," she sighed. "And like you, I am limited on what I can do here. I am also in a cage. But your destiny is not tied to this spot forever."

"I'm so unbelievably tired of this destiny thing," I groaned. "Can someone please just tell me what my purpose is since everyone seems to know it but me?"

"You haven't been listening," Medea chuckled. "Your job is to live. Like the first humans, your soul's purpose is to protect and honor life here on this plane of existence."

"And how do I do that? Everyone just wants to go to the realm. How do I make them stay?" As soon as the words left my mouth, I knew exactly what I needed to do. I wasn't sure if Medea put the thought in my head, or if I was just too hardheaded to figure it out before now.

"How?" I turned to ask her. "How can I do it? I can't take down every portal in the world."

She placed her long leathery fingers on my forearm. "You don't need to take them all down."

"Can I really do this?" My eyes widened in a hopeful excitement.

"You are the only one who can." Medea returned my smile. "I'll give you the tools you need, but you are the only one that will be able to make it work."

"What will happen to the people who aren't spirits in the realm?" I glanced over to the kitchen window and saw the outline of Freida by the sink.

"There is a failsafe at each major system operating center. If damage occurs at the site, anyone wearing trackers connected to the system will be pulled out while the reboot takes place. Once they are safe, your work begins." Medea pulled the pendant from her neck and draped the long chain over my head.

"This is for strength." Her voice soothed me as the heavy pendant settled against my chest. "The words will be the power."

I nodded as I memorized the words she whispered in my ear. *This was a destiny I could live with.*

*

"Are you truly ready for this?" Vorie sat cross-legged on my bedroom floor as I packed my bag with a few items I owned. Not that I actually owned much, most of it was a gift. The irony wasn't lost on me.

"I don't have another choice," I sighed while zipping the bag. "This is my destiny. The one you wouldn't just come out and tell me about."

"You know I couldn't do that." I could hear her smiling through her words. "The only time you really figure something out is when you learn the hard way."

I watched as the weak rays of dawn lit up the frosted window. The previous night felt dreamlike and blurry. *The ancient language Medea spoke into my ear in the mystical darkness of the courtyard. It seemed so simple, but now in the breaking light of day...*

I pushed the doubt away. It had to work. We didn't have another option.

"Well I figured it out now." I turned to face Vorie.

"If they find out it was you everyone will hate you for this. No one will forgive you for what you're about to do." Vorie's ghostly eyes shimmered with tears. I'd known her long enough to understand she was just trying to protect me, trying to save me from further pain.

141

"I'm willing to deal with those consequences." I slung the strap of my pack over my shoulders. "Just please let Genie know I'll be there in a few hours and make sure she brings Fergus." Vorie nodded.

"I'm surprised you didn't sneak out in the middle of the night," she laughed, attempting to lighten the somber mood.

I opened my bedroom door and heard Freida bustling into the kitchen to start her morning shift. "I'm trying to do things right this time," I smiled and gave her one of my famously horrible winks. "You should be proud. I learned that from you."

*

"Where are you going?" Freida's red rimmed eyes glanced to the pack I was wearing.

"There is something important I have to do. I'm on my way to see Alister now." I waited as she hung up her sweater and pulled the apron down from the peg.

"No more trouble I hope." She arched an eyebrow in my direction as she tied the strings around her hips.

"That I don't know," I shrugged playfully, not wanting to lie but also not wanting to add to her stress. I crossed the stone kitchen floor and wrapped my arms around her.

"I'm going to fix the world for you," I whispered.

"What was that?" Freida asked as she pulled back from the embrace. "I didn't hear what you said."

"Nothing important," I smiled warmly. "I just wanted to let you know that everything will be okay."

"Hurry back then so I don't worry." She went to light the stove.

"I'll try," I said softly, pausing at the kitchen door. "And Freida…" She turned to look at me. "I think Odan will be back soon." Her eyes lit up with hope and that's all I needed to push me through the door.

There was a note in my bedroom for the professor saying my good-byes if I didn't make it back. He was a good man, even if he was in his own head most of the time, but I didn't want to wait to speak with him. *Who knows how long it'll take his magic beans to kick in?*

"Take me to Alister's office please," I told the guards as I slipped into the backseat. The gray morning fog never lifted as we drove deeper into the district. I nervously wrung my hands as I watched the clouds.

It was probably going to snow again, but that didn't fill me with wonder. The people in the city would be cold and more would go to the realm soon.

It would have been easier to sneak away. I pushed away the thought. I owed it to Alister to explain what was happening. My heart ached as I searched for the right words to say. He wouldn't be able to help. They'd never let him go. *Well then, I at least need to tell him good-bye.* I hardened my resolve as I stared at the passing sky.

*

"Will you drive me to Genie's house?"

Alister sat at his desk and looked up to me with heavy eyes. The blueprints were hastily shoved into a folder when I entered. I pretended not to notice the edges of the paper peeking out.

"I'm not sure that's a good idea. We'd need to organize a large escort to go to the plantation."

"Not there," I shook my head. "Her old house. It's outside the city limits."

"Do we need to go now?" He glanced down at the work on his desk.

I adjusted the strap of my bag. "Yes Alister. This is important. There are some things I need to tell you and I'm trying to do this the right way this time."

I don't know if it was the strain in my voice or if he sensed things were about to change, but he didn't argue as he wearily stood up from his desk.

The guards agreed to follow behind Alister's Honda. As we backed out of the parking spot, I watched Reynolds give us a curious look before scurrying into the building.

"I hate that guy," I mumbled under my breath.

"I'm not too fond of him either." Alister put the transmission into drive.

I reached over to hold his hand as he drove us out of the city and explained everything Medea had told me. He listened in silence until I finished.

"I don't know why we are going to see Genie. The mafia isn't going to help. There is too much as stake for them."

"It's not the mafia's help I need," I smiled. The clouds above the trees grew darker.

"It's too dangerous." He clenched the muscles in his jaw as he slowed down the car. "There has to be another way."

I gave his hand a loving squeeze. "You and I both know there isn't."

*

The smoke curled from the chimney of the tiny house with a green door tucked between two industrial buildings. I smiled despite the circumstances. Genie was already there.

145

The guards waited in their vehicle as Alister and I walked up the steps. I lifted the knocker and the door was yanked open out of my hands.

"No freaking way is this happening." Genie stood blocking the doorway with her arms folded across her chest.

"Is Vorie here?" I tried to look over Genie's head into the living room. She huffed as she stepped aside to let us in. Vorie and Craton were sitting on the couch. Fergus leaned against the back wall.

"What is he doing here?" Alister growled when he saw Fergus.

I held his hand firmly. "I asked him to come. I need his help."

"This is suicide." Genie threw her hands in the air after she bolted the door. "Everyone will hate us and hunt us down." I peered through the blinds. The guards were still in their car with the heater running.

"Did you tell her what they were planning to do?" I asked Vorie.

She nodded as Genie screamed, "Then why don't we just destroy the new technology instead of taking the realm away from us all?"

"It's not that simple." I turned toward her. "It's bigger than just a single device. Everyone around the world is racing to be the first to complete it. I

146

might be able to take a few attempts down, but how long before they murder me, and I can't stop it anymore?" Genie paled as Craton pulled her onto his lap.

"This is the only way to save us all and I'm not taking the realm from you. It will still be there when it's your time to go."

Craton wrapped his arms around his wife. "We are going to help. What do you need us to do?"

*

First things first, I'd need an organized series of damages to occur targeting the system bases infrastructure to set off the safety protocol and pull everyone in the realm out. Craton and Fergus hastily wrote up a list of the major ones.

New York, Brazil, Sydney, London, Cairo, Hyderabad, Tokyo… *Talk about convenient.*

Then I'd have a four-hour window to get to a support center, but I'd deal with that part later.

"And where do you suppose we will find a worldwide network of people to work together?" Alister asked as he looked over the list. Vorie, Genie, and I smiled.

"I think we can find some people," I smirked.

"Even if you get a bunch of orphans together," Craton sighed. "It's going to be hard to get them to all want to help. Not everyone hates the realm."

"Luckily for us, I know someone who specializes in that kind of thing. We just have to arrange the meeting there." *I was going to see the Ruby Mountains again.*

Alister stepped outside to make a phone call. His job was to convince the board that in order to keep me out of trouble, I was being sent on an embassy mission to the Pacific Northwest to request that the towns join the country. Since I'd lived among the people, there was hope that I could end the long-standing rebellion.

Fergus came over to the sofa as I was writing a list of people who would potentially join our cause.

"I have some friends in Egypt and Japan," he said softly. "They are destroyers like me. They'll take care of those bases for you."

"Thank you," I smiled up at him. "If Genie gets the girl who replaced her from South India on board, we should have everything covered."

"Is there anything else I can do to help?" he asked.

I looked around the room. Vorie and Craton were in the kitchen convincing Genie not to panic. Alister was still outside on the phone.

"That information that I asked you for," I whispered. "I'm still going to need it."

*

Once the plans were finalized, I burned every piece of paper we'd used in the woodstove. I hugged Genie and promised her it would be okay. I'd build a fashion house in the realm just for her the minute we both went for real. She sulked, but I saw her eyes brighten at the prospect.

Our good-byes were laced with a heavy tension as we all went our separate ways. Vorie was headed to New York. Genie and Craton were going to Brazil and then India. Fergus was going to talk to his buddies. We were all to meet up in the Northern Nevada desert in three days. That would give me just enough time to find Lilith and have her contact Karl before I had to go beg for Juniper's help.

149

Chapter 13

∞

"How will we find her?" I asked.

Alister refused to leave my side until I was safely back in the village. He told the guards we needed to have some fun, so they stayed dutifully in the shadows as we entered the realm.

"Listen for the siren's song," Alister laughed sarcastically.

"What does that even mean?" I rolled my eyes.

"Nothing," he shook his head. "Just a bad joke. I already called in her location." The guards stepped forward to touch our shoulders as we manifested away.

*

"Where are we?" I asked.

A soothing mist filled the air and the sound of rushing water mixed with the delicate hum of a distant harp. Alister turned me around to see a waterfall pouring down a mountain slope. Pools of steaming water sat nestled within circles of river rock.

"The baths," he explained. "They are supposed to be relaxing." We walked the grassy path between the boulders until we came to the first pool.

"Excuse us," Alister muttered politely to the group of young men reclining in the crystal-clear water.

"She should be in the next one," he said as he grabbed my hand and led me deeper into the mist.

"Fawn!" Lilith exclaimed as we approached the water's edge. "What on earth are you doing here?"

She stood from the pool and the water rolled in rivulets off her naked body. I nervously glanced at Alister, but his attention was fixated on his shoes.

"Can I speak with you for a minute?" I asked, trying to avoid looking at her... um... assets.

"Of course," she laughed and reached for a towel despite the groans of her male companions.

"I need your help. Can you meet me somewhere in two days? I'll get you the credits for your ticket."

"Outside the realm?" She looked curiously at me.

I nodded. "And are you still in touch with Karl? I need him to come too."

"I can do that," she said in confusion. "What's this all about? Is it something to do with The Nocere?"

"It's so much more than that." I looked over at the men in the pool. Their eyes were fixated on Lilith. "I can't explain now. Just promise you'll come."

"I promise," she smiled. "Orphans stick together."

Alister gave her some credits and the coded location to the Placeville portal.

"That's going to look great on the budget ledger," Alister sighed as he guided us to the exit. "I wonder how I'll explain that I just paid some random siren in the baths."

*

"Wait out here," Alister commanded the guards as we entered the portal hall. "I want to speak with Miss Vita in private for a moment."

The guards gave each other a subtle look and I felt myself blush. Alister shook his head as he closed the door behind us.

"I'll be okay," I sighed. "You don't have to lecture me before I go."

"It's not that." He reached for my hand and I felt the familiar surge of sensation that we alone shared in the realm. "I want to come with you."

I stared at his face and willed myself not to cry. "You know that's not possible. Not only will it raise suspicion, your place is there and not with me right now."

"My soul says differently," he smiled mischievously. "It believes I belong with you."

"Then there is nothing to worry about." I tugged his arm to wrap it around my back. "We will always be tied together."

"And what if something happens to you?" He pulled me closer to him. "How would I live?"

"The world doesn't revolve around the two of us."

"Well maybe it should," he groaned.

"You don't mean that. There will be a lot of confused and angry people looking for guidance. They'll need your leadership more than ever. You cannot come."

"I know," he sighed. "That day in the boardroom, Medea whispered to me too. She said that the time would come when we'd need to separate, and I needed to be okay with that. Just know that I am not okay."

"I promise I'll be careful." I turned my face up to his.

The fear of the unknown and the immediate longing softened his features making him appear vulnerable. I stood on my toes and parted his lips with mine, kissing him deeply. I wanted to give him strength to face whatever was about to happen. There was so much more to say, but I couldn't stay. Time was running out. I pulled my lips away.

"Promise you'll come back," he whispered with his eyes closed. I wanted to lie, wanted to promise him the moon and stars, anything to make this parting easier.

"We will always find each other." I stepped out of his arms and bit my lip to keep it from quivering. He stood still as a statue watching me leave. I touched the pendant hanging under my shirt, needing some strength too.

The ache grew stronger with every step I took, but destiny is a bitch and doesn't care what anyone wants. I made it to the portal without breaking down and raised my arm to the panel.

The void instantly ripped me away and although part of me stayed there with him, the part that was left smiled. I was going home.

*

The desert breeze was chilling as it whipped my hair around my face. I hastily tied it back. The abandoned cars still lined the streets outside the theatre portal. I remembered how haunting it seemed the first time I saw it. Like an entire town abandoned them here and just walked into the portal one day, never to return. Now I was grateful for them. We'd need a lot of transportation soon.

I checked the old truck nearest to the portal. The keys fell from the visor when I lowered it. Smiling at my luck, I started the engine. It did take a few tries and some choice words, but I finally got it going.

I followed the highway in the direction the mafia had driven into the town from. When I saw the outskirts of Fallon's farm my heart grew lighter. I wanted to stop and say hello, but the sun was going down and I knew it was almost time for dinner.

The familiar smells and sounds of the hotel greeted me from the kitchen as I stepped into the lobby.

"Just a minute," Mrs. Shaw called from the table as the bell on the door chimed above me.

"Don't worry. I've got it." Brayson walked into the lobby to see me standing there. My cheeks burned from how big I was smiling. I ran to his arms with a silencing finger pressed against my lips.

"Fawn," he gasped as he squeezed me tightly in a hug. "What are you doing here?"

"Vorie didn't warn you?" I asked through whispered giggles. "I figured she would have."

"No." He stared at me in disbelief. "You look so different now."

"Me?" I stepped back to inspect him. "You are huge! It seems like they've been working you hard and feeding you well." I playfully tapped his stomach. Brayson smiled.

"Who is it, son?" Mr. Shaw called.

"Just a hungry orphan city girl looking for a free meal," I joked as I stepped around Brayson's widened frame and into the kitchen. "Got any food to spare?"

Once Oleen stopped shrieking, Mrs. Shaw got her random bursts of tears under control, and Mr. Shaw released me from his too tight embrace, I sat on the worn wooden chair cushion and loaded up my plate.

"I missed your cooking so much," I groaned as I took another bite of the casserole.

"Where have you been? Have they not been feeding you? You look too skinny." Mrs. Shaw practically threw the breadbasket at me.

I thought of Freida and smiled. The two of them could have been friends in another life. Well, they might tear each other's hair out, but they were more alike than I thought.

"I've been in D.C. The government's capital city," I said. "The food isn't as good as yours, but yes, they feed me." Mrs. Shaw gave me a triumphant smile.

"Have those con artist government cronies been treating you okay?" Mr. Shaw raised his fork threateningly in the air.

"Actually," I grimaced as I sank deeper into the chair. "I kind of work for them now." The room was so silent you could hear a pin drop.

"But don't worry," I hastily added. "I'm not here because of that."

*

My room in the hotel was left untouched. I ran my hands over my clothes in the drawer. These things were mine, not gifts, but things I'd picked out with my own hands.

"She wouldn't throw them out and wouldn't let anyone in here," Brayson said as he walked into the room. "I wanted to tell her you might not come back, but I didn't want to break her heart. Here you are though, proving me wrong."

"I'm sorry I left without saying goodbye." I hugged myself as I watched him walk across the room to sit on the sofa. "I didn't want to go."

"It's alright," he shrugged. "Vorie explained everything. And to be honest, if you wouldn't have left the way you did then I would have had to come with you. So, thanks for leaving." He gave me a playful grin.

"Don't be rude."

Brayson's eyes lit up as Vorie manifested beside him.

"Me? Rude?" he smiled. "Never. Maybe you're the rude one for not telling me she was coming."

"I wanted it to be a surprise," Vorie giggled.

I couldn't help but smile as I saw the two of them together. It was almost like old times, but they couldn't touch, and I noticed the yearning in their practiced movements as they spoke. They were together, but not fully. Not able to be in each other's world. I pushed the ache to see Alister deep down into the recesses of my heart. We would all need to make sacrifices for the greater good.

"Earth to Fawn," Vorie laughed.

"I'm sorry. What were you saying?" I shook my head, letting the thoughts fall away.

"I was asking what the plan is." Brayson gave me a concerned look.

"Oh that," I sighed. "First, I need to talk to Juniper tomorrow…"

*

I didn't need to look for Juniper. She came to the hotel after breakfast. It shouldn't have surprised me, nothing in that town happened without her knowing.

"Can we take a walk?" I asked as I dried the final pot Mrs. Shaw handed me from the sink. "There is something I need to talk to you about."

"I'm glad you're back," Juniper said once we stepped outside. "But something tells me this isn't a friendly visit."

"It's not." I shook my head and kept quiet until we reached the end of Main Street, away from prying eyes and potential eavesdroppers.

"They are going to use the technology from The Nocere to trap incoming spirits," I hurriedly explained. "A witch named Medea gave me what I need to stop this, but we have to organize a widespread attack on the system before I can do it." Juniper bit her lip as she studied the barren desert landscape.

"When you told me about the grates, I wondered how far they would take something like that," she sighed. "What do you need me to do?"

Relief washed over me. I was taking a risk by coming here without speaking to her first, but she was the only person I knew who could bring so many hardheaded people together to work toward a common goal.

"I just need you to get everyone on board. They should start arriving tomorrow. I'll head back to the portal today and leave instructions on how to get here. Then I'll make sure there are enough working vehicles parked out front."

Juniper nodded as she listened to the plan. "We'll need to hold a town meeting tonight."

I lowered my head as I put my hands in my pockets. "Do we really have to? I've already brought so much drama here. I'm not so sure they'll be happy to see me, just to learn I'm bringing more. I promise this is just a meeting spot for one day and then everyone will leave."

"There are no secret meetings in this town," she said as she turned to face me. "Complete transparency is the only way there can be trust."

I remembered Theo sitting on the sidewalk crying after he told the mafia I was there. She must have seen the worry on my face.

"No one is going to give you away," she said. "Theo has moved on. But just to be on the safe side, we won't give them all the details. A little discretion might be okay." I thanked her as we headed back to town.

"Why don't you stop by Fallon's farm on your way to the portal today? There is someone who might want to come with you." Juniper gave me a sly smile.

*

The truck started easily, and I headed down the familiar dirt roads to the farm. Winter had dropped the leaves from some trees, but the pines stayed green and full. The fields were empty as I drove past them. It looked so much different than it did in the summer, but I knew it would be alive again the following year. That thought made me happy.

I turned the truck down the driveway that led to the main house. Fallon parked his tractor and swung his aging body down in one agile leap.

"Is that really you?" He spit a wad of tobacco on the ground and I skipped past it as I raced to hug him.

"Let me see you," he laughed as he held me at arm's distance. "You look like you've gone soft. We'll need to toughen you up again."

He kept his arm around me, steering me toward the greenhouses, as he talked about the final

161

harvest of the season and the new aquatic system he built for the indoor planting this winter. I swelled with pride at all he'd done and regretted not being here to help.

"This is the one that took your place," he said as he opened the door. "It was a rough start, but she's doing well now. Maybe even a harder worker than you are."

A curtain of jet-black hair adorned the girl who stood tending the seedlings at the back of the greenhouse.

"Astrid?" I gasped. She spun around and her very normal starless black eyes met mine.

"You're alive!" she shrieked as she ran toward me. Fallon backed out of the room to give us space to reconnect.

"Make sure you're here at 6 o'clock tomorrow morning," he said to Astrid. She looked to both of us in confusion.

"Come on," I laughed as I grabbed her hand. "He's giving you the rest of the day off."

*

"How did you get here? What happened?" I was giddy as I climbed behind the steering wheel. One glance at her arm told me I didn't need to ask why she was no longer in service.

162

"It was the strangest thing," she gave me a sarcastic smile. "Someone told Juniper there was a girl that looked just like her at the Seattle orphanage and she came to investigate. Turns out, she's my cousin. Well, second cousin maybe. She was related to my biological mother somehow. She asked me if I wanted to leave and I wasn't about to say no."

Astrid paused as she looked out the window. "It's a nice enough place here, do you miss it? Brayson told me how you had to leave."

At the mention of his name, I cast a side eye in her direction. "Do you spend a lot of time with him?"

"A little," she shrugged.

Protectiveness of Vorie and the desire for Brayson's happiness rocked me with discomfort. I gripped the wheel tighter as I drove.

"Do you like him?"

"What's not to like?" Astrid sighed. "But he is pretty much married to Vorie." I breathed easier knowing we were on the same page.

"Well I have a surprise for you," I smiled. "Guess who else is coming to visit tomorrow?"

Chapter 14

∞

The town gathered for the emergency meeting that night. I was nervous when I walked inside, but I didn't need to be. Warm hugs and strong claps on the back greeted me as I entered. Still, I held my breath as Juniper addressed the room with the topic for discussion.

"There is a situation within the realm. I can't disclose all the details, but Fawn has a plan to fix it. She asked to use this hall and my mediator skills to go over this plan with a group of individuals that will help her handle the situation. Discretion is key here, but as per our rules every action taken in this town gets a vote. I won't lie and say this won't bring danger here, because it might, but I strongly believe we are doing the right thing by helping. What say you?"

There was a steady buzz of whispers as the townsfolk talked among themselves. I twisted my hands in my lap as I waited for their vote. Mrs. Shaw wrapped her arm around me and gave me a comforting smile. A deeply wrinkled man wearing a cowboy hat stood from his chair.

"You called us here for this?" he asked. His raised voice silenced the conversation. I felt my heart drop as he turned and pointed to me. "Fawn is one of us. Whatever she needs she can have. There was no need to ask. You want secrecy? Well then, I didn't see or hear nothing. Neither did anyone else in this room."

There were nods of approval from all the attendants as they closed their eyes and said their "ayes."

"Opposed?" Juniper smirked. Dead silence. "Meeting adjourned then," she smiled at me from across the room.

*

"What was that about?" I asked Brayson after he'd lingered a few minutes longer with Astrid at the door to the empty meeting house.

"Nothing," he shrugged. "She's just nice to talk to. Vorie would have liked her a lot."

"Would have?" I blew out a steamy breath and watched the cloud drift up to the starry night. The desert skies were unlike any other. "She can still meet her. It's not like she's gone forever."

"You know what I mean." He nudged me with his shoulder as we crossed the street.

*

"Did you see Brayson tonight?" I asked nonchalantly as Vorie's ghostly form laid beside me on the bed.

"Not yet," she smiled. "I wanted to check on you first. How are you feeling about being back here? I know you missed it."

"It's different." I rolled on my side to face her. "I love it here, but it's like they moved on without me. Maybe that doesn't make sense, because I know they had to keep living, but it just kind of feels like this isn't where I belong."

"It's not," Vorie said softly. "Not anymore."

"Yeah. I figured as much," I sighed. "Did you know the girl I worked with at The Nocere, Astrid, is here?"

"I've heard her name once or twice," Vorie smiled, but I saw the hidden pain in the way she swallowed her breath.

"I'll take care of this." The muscles in my jaw clenched. My fears were written on the wall and I'd be damned if I let Brayson hurt Vorie. *That rat bastard.*

"No, you won't." She snuggled closer to me. "I've been the one encouraging it. He deserves to be happy."

"And you don't?" My eyes opened wide in outrage.

"I am happy. This will make me happier. Now let's walk through the plan for tomorrow…"

*

Brayson and Astrid stood outside the hotel the following morning waiting for me. I made sure to walk between them despite the lecture from Vorie. I might not be able to stop what was happening, but I didn't have to see it.

We went to check the town hall, where we'd be hanging out for the next few hours as we waited for our guests. I smiled as we entered the building. The townsfolk promised ignorance to the meeting about to take place, but the table set up in the back of the room holding baskets of snacks and drinks said differently. Their silent support gave me confidence.

Genie and Fergus were the first to arrive. Two body builders trailed in after them.

"Where's Craton?" I asked as I greeted her with a hug.

"We decided it would be best if he wasn't involved," she whispered in my ear. "What's that about?" she asked, motioning to Brayson and Astrid laughing over the snack table.

"Ask Vorie," I sighed. Genie moseyed over dramatically to Brayson, fawning over him and casting a suspicious eye to Astrid which caused me to giggle.

"Hey," I looked to Fergus as he approached me. "Were you able to get the information that I asked for?"

"I was," he nodded. "It's the support center in L.A."

"Perfect," I said. "I can just ask Brayson where it is, and this will all work out." The body builders stepped closer to us.

"Are these your friends?" I asked, pointing to the men.

"This is Adofo and Kaito." He waved them forward. "I've already discussed the plan with them. They are on board."

"Just let us know when," Kaito said as he lowered his head. Adofo nodded, giving me the most delicious smile, which made me nervously look away. *Maybe I should introduce him to Astrid.*

"Fergus," Brayson said, suddenly beside me, and holding out his hand. "It's nice to see you again. Sorry I put you in a box."

"No harm done." Fergus gave him a firm handshake. "If I were in your shoes, I probably would have done the same thing."

"Is this the guy that bested you?" Kaito and Adofo teased. Fergus shoved them back and the three of them headed to the food table laughing.

The double doors opened wide and the little pixie girl who I'd met at Vorie's end of service party came strolling through. On each side of her, like two

168

protective lions, stood Claire and Chloe. They fussed over the girl's hair as she shooed them away.

"Fawn!" the twins shrieked in unison as they hustled the girl over to me. "What is this all about? Sammy has been throwing a fit since your friend Vorie begged her to come and we couldn't stop her."

Sammy smiled up at me as she crossed her arms. "We are here to help," she nodded before turning toward the food. The twins gave me a quick hug as they rushed to follow the girl.

She has them wrapped around her finger, I laughed to myself. *Good for her.*

Next came Damini, Genie's replacement when her contract ended, with her brother Drishith at her side. They looked anxiously around the room and Genie tried to make them feel welcome.

My face lit up when Lane entered hand in hand with the very handsome bouncer from Dives.

"How are you?" I asked as I led them into the room. The smile on his sun kissed face mirrored my own.

"The best I've ever been." He gave me a gentle hug. "That was actually my first time in the realm in months."

"What?" My jaw dropped.

"Well Tony here keeps me busy," he laughed as he squeezed his date's hand.

Relief washed over me. I figured that Lane would be the hardest one to convince.

"So, you won't mind if we tear it all down?" I whispered in his ear.

Lane shook his head with a devious smile. "Genie already told me. I'm ready. We don't need the damn thing anyway."

I returned his conspiratorial grin as Brayson came to speak with him. I hadn't noticed Juniper come in, but I caught sight of her sitting in the back shadows of the room.

"Oh good, you're here," I said as I walked over to her. "We are just waiting on…"

The doors flew open as Lilith entered. Her red hair shined brighter with more gold in the real light and her freckles popped, giving her face a sultry, classically beautiful sweetness. Karl ambled in behind her and closed the door. His belly had grown since the last time I saw him.

"Let's get started," Juniper said as she stretched out her neck. "You take the lead. I'm only here to help."

*

I stood in the center of the room and asked everyone to take a seat. I knew that orphans don't rat each other out, so I wasn't worried about getting caught, but I was nervous because this plan needed to work. There was no plan B.

I laid out the details and what they needed to do before opening the floor for discussion. Once the initial shock and anger wore off, I could instantly see who was on board and who wasn't.

"Crap." I looked to Juniper for help.

"You're doing fine," she whispered back.

"It's too dangerous," Claire shook her head. "You could get hurt."

"Either I'm doing it or you're doing it," Sammy glared. "I don't care about the danger."

"But think of all the fun we have in the realm. We wouldn't get to have that anymore," Chloe tried to reason with the girl.

"I don't ever want to go back there again," Sammy stood her ground.

"I know everyone will miss the excitement of the realm, but it's not going anywhere. We will all end up there eventually. Think of it as something to look forward to," I explained. "And if we worked here in the world, we could make our own exciting places too."

"And what about our mother?" Drishith asked. "We would never be able to visit her. She died when we were young, we would have never gotten to know her without the realm."

"Hush," Damini commanded her brother. "You know she doesn't like us to come there anyway. But what is there to stop this from happening again as soon as the portals reboot?"

"That is my job," I reassured her. "I have a way to destroy the entire system." She nodded her head in agreement and her brother reluctantly did the same.

"We have less to worry about," Karl said as he leaned back in his chair. "Although they'll come for all of us, I'm no longer in service. What about the ones still under contract? You of all people know what happens if you disobey. If this fails, the punishment will be brutal."

I bit my lip as I looked to my feet. That was my biggest fear too. Doubts came crashing into me again. This wasn't going to work.

"Then we don't fail." Juniper came to stand beside me.

"The stakes are too high. If we do this, and succeed, it isn't about just letting us live freely in the afterlife. Bringing this system down stops mothers from abandoning their children when they run to the realm. It takes away the jobs from orphans and gets them out of the mafia's hands. It stops the decay of humanity and brings life back to the way it should be. And it prevents the corrupt and powerful from taking even more. Death, and the realm, are our equalizers. No one should have the power to change that."

I watched Lilith's eyes change during Juniper's speech. My heart broke for her when I remembered her punishment and added sentence was because she'd tried to find her birth parents in the realm.

"This is a stupid plan," Lilith sighed. "But I'm in. At least if we die now, we can make it to the realm before they trap our spirits. Eternity as a slave sounds like an even shittier plan than this one."

"Finally!" Sammy exclaimed and the room erupted with laughter.

"When do we start?" Karl asked as the humor died down.

"Twenty-four hours," I smiled.

*

Genie explained where the major tech center locations were according to the information Craton laid out and Brayson described where the damage needed to occur to set off the safety protocol. The results should be instant. The minute the warning was triggered, it would pull all users out of the realm and send them spiraling back to their respective portals.

Then I'd have the short window to do my job before the system was rebooted.

We had the advantage of surprise. Medea explained that no one in many years had attempted to mess with the portal technology. The techs had become complacent. That was fine by me. I didn't want anyone to get hurt.

True, I could have left them in the realm and waited to see what happened once I shut down the system, but it was risky. We knew this way would be safe and save as many people as we could. Not like we knew it for a fact or anything.

I sat down in the chair and my mind drifted to the time I'd yelled at Alister for pulling me through the portal without a tracker. Unconsciously, I ran my thumb over the star pendant I wore. *Trust. I have to trust this will work.*

"It's time," Fergus said as he placed a hand on my shoulder. Everyone was getting ready to leave and head back to their corners of the earth to do some serious damage.

"Thank you all for helping." I held open the door.

"That's what we do," Sammy said as she skipped down the steps with Claire and Chloe racing to keep up. "Orphans take care of each other."

*

"You ready to go?"

I grabbed my backpack and filled it with the belongings I'd missed when I left the first time. Taking one last look around the hotel room, I sighed and closed my eyes. *No. I'm not ready.*

"You can come back," Brayson chuckled. "No need to get all sentimental."

"Maybe one day." I gave him a sad smile as I pulled the pack over my shoulder. "You know you don't have to come, right?"

"And miss the final showdown? Not a chance. Plus, you can't shoot for shit and I'm the only one here who has actually been to the support facility. Hell, I used to work there. But I don't know why we have to go to that one when Juniper says the one in Portland is closer."

"It has to be that one. And that's all the more reason why you shouldn't come. They might remember you." I rolled my eyes and pushed him out of my path.

"Fawn stop."

I did.

"Listen, what you are doing is for the best, but it takes me permanently away from Vorie. I'll never be able to visit her, never see her on my own terms. It'll be a lifetime before I get to hold her again. I'd been toying with the idea of getting another

175

tracker, but I wanted to wait until I was strong enough to come back to the real world. Now I won't have that choice. I know it's for the greater good and I'm okay with it. But I've got Vorie whispering in one ear, and I can see on your face that you are angry about it too. And Astrid is so…" his voice trailed off and he ran a hand through his too long hair.

"My brain is all mixed up, but I need to help. I need it to be my choice and I have to do something to fix everything that's happened. I'm coming with you, okay?"

Tears welled in the corners of my eyes and I nodded. For the first time since she'd left, I sensed Vorie standing next to me and holding my hand even though I couldn't see her there.

"You deserve to be happy," I said. "And if being stubborn brings you joy, fine. Let's go."

*

Genie and Fergus were waiting for us outside on the sidewalk.

"I still don't understand why we can't just use the portal," Genie sighed. "We might as well get one last use out of it before it disappears."

"You didn't tell her?" I raised an eyebrow at Fergus.

"She wouldn't let me get a word in," he shrugged.

"Genie," I said as I reached for her hand. "You're not coming with us. We'll drop you off at the portal and you can take it home."

"No." She pulled her hand away. "I'm not leaving you again. This is our fight, not just yours."

"I need you to go home so we don't raise suspicion." I pulled her back. "If anyone finds out it was me that did this I'll be hunted for the rest of my life. I need you to go back and pretend everything is normal. I'm not taking the portal so there won't be any trace of me showing up there. As far as anyone knows, I'm on an embassy mission. If they find out I was in L.A., or if they see that both of us are gone when the portals crash, someone is bound to connect the dots. I can't risk you getting hurt."

"Why are you being this way?" Genie glared at me through tear glossed eyes. "There's a chance I'll never see you again. I'm not ready to let that happen."

"Worst case?" I gave her a sly smile, hoping to keep the fear from my voice. "I'll see you in the realm. But if this works out like I think it will, everything will be okay."

"No," she stomped her foot on the ground. "I should have gone with you the first time you left. I'm not making the same mistake twice."

"Please," I begged as I wrapped my arms around her. "I shouldn't have asked the first time. It wasn't right of me to rip you away from your life and it's not right of me to do it now. I need you to be safe so I don't worry, and if something happens to me, I'll need you to take care of Alister."

"You just said nothing will happen." She wiped a hand angrily over her eyes. I placed my forehead against hers. "Fine," she snapped as she pulled away. "Don't be stupid and come back safe."

Juniper drove her Jeep down Main Street and parked beside us.

"I don't need a ride from you." Genie stormed off down the road. "I'll find my own way."

"Should I go after her?" Fergus asked.

"No." I shook my head and blinked to keep the tears from falling. "She'll be alright. This is just how she copes with things."

*

"Are you sure you want to come too?" I asked Juniper as I climbed into the passenger seat. "This is a risk you don't have to take, and the town needs you here."

Juniper rolled her eyes. "Just get in and buckle up. You can't shoot. You can't fight. I'm not sending you to the wolves alone."

I clutched the pendant in my hand and smiled. The heavy warmth spread through my fingers. *Maybe not,* I thought. *But I'm still going to save the world.*

Chapter 15

∞

We drove through the night, down the same highways that Brayson and I once drove on in what seemed like a lifetime ago. I nodded off once or twice. Juniper told me to take a shift so she could close her eyes. That scared me more than anything else about the trip. She didn't say anything, but I got the feeling that if I damaged her Jeep, I'd be safer on the wrong side of the mafia.

I thought everyone was sound asleep when Fergus touched my shoulder, scaring the hell out of me.

"Are you sure about this?" he whispered in my ear after my heart rate returned to normal. "When Brayson finds out what you are doing he is going to lose it. We should wait for someone else to be there."

"No," I sighed. "It has to be him. They'll blame whoever was working that shift. He is the only person I know who deserves that kind of punishment. To be on the safe side though, we can't let Brayson come inside."

*

"How will we know if it worked?" Brayson yawned loudly, pulling me from my light sleep. The imprint of the side panel was pressed into my face. I rubbed away the tingling sensation as I opened my eyes.

Towering palm trees loomed over the abandoned concrete jungle. We were entering L.A.

"Can we head downtown first?" I asked as I looked at the crumbling buildings. A sense of dread was gathering in my stomach. I didn't know what I would feel coming back to the area I'd lived most of my life, but this overwhelming urge to run took me by surprise.

"Lead the way," Juniper yawned.

Brayson leaned forward and began pointing out directions. His voice was strained, and I could tell he felt the same way I did.

We snaked deeper into the city, turning down old and familiar roads. The horror of our childhood and pain from the night Vorie died was almost palpable as we entered our old neighborhood. I closed my eyes when we passed 17th Street.

"There." I pointed at the old coffee shop where our portal was. On the broken sidewalk was a cluster of people. Some staggered as they held to the brick wall. Others stepped into the street, shading their eyes from the blinding morning sun and tripping over the wasted bodies of those who'd been in the realm for too long.

In the middle of the crowd I saw Ruth holding a backpack. Her brow was creased in concern as she counted out the water bottles she had. I held the pendant in my hand as I watched her begin propping up the Can't Commits. Hope replaced the gut-wrenching dread, and I felt strong again.

"Should we stop?" Juniper asked as we slowly cruised past the scene.

"It's alright," I said, sliding down lower in the seat so she wouldn't see me through the window. "Ruth will take care of them and Kramer will help. The orphans did their job. Now it's time for me to do mine."

*

Juniper parked the Jeep in the alley across the street from the building covered in glass windows. There were so many levels I wasn't sure we'd ever figure out where to go.

"Are you sure this is the place?" I asked.

"I worked here for two years," Brayson said. "I'm positive this is it. The first two floors are the architects. The third floor is where the computer techs work."

Well I guess that narrows it down.

"You need to stay here," I told him. "We can't risk someone recognizing you."

"That's not going to happen." Brayson unbuckled his seatbelt. "If we go through the side entrance, we can avoid the architects completely."

"And what happens when we accidently bump into someone?" I glared at him. "How will you explain what you are doing here?"

"Fawn. We talked about this. I'm coming to help." He returned my glare.

"She's right." Juniper turned off the engine. "We are here for backup. You have thirty minutes and if you aren't done by then, we are coming in with guns blazing."

Brayson leaned back and muttered something under his breath, but I knew he wouldn't argue with Juniper. She reached under her seat and pulled out the 9mm, then placed it in my hand.

"Get close enough that you don't have to worry about missing," she smiled. I tucked the pistol into my waistband. It was a lot heavier than I remembered.

*

"I really hope this works," I said to Fergus as we hurried across the street.

"Me too," he chuckled. "I don't want to see what Juniper looks like in a fight."

The side entrance led to a dark stairwell and we quickly climbed three flights of stairs without seeing another living soul.

"What if he is out sick today?" My heart was thudding against my chest and my thoughts were racing. *This is stupid. How am I just supposed to use some words to end this? This a bad plan...* I clutched the star pendant Medea gave me. *For strength.* The mantra ran through my head again. *Trust that it will be okay.*

"I don't know." Fergus' lips were in a thin line. "He was the only one on the schedule today. We just have to hope this all works out." He placed his hand on the bar of the heavy metal door. "Are you ready?"

"I have to be," I nodded.

*

"Who are you?" a woman gasped in a shrill voice as the door swung open. Fergus' broad shoulders filled the doorway, blocking my view of her.

"I think I'm lost," he shrugged with his palms up.

The sound of the voice came from the office to the right of the stairwell exit. As he stepped into the hall, I slipped out from behind him, staying in his shadow to avoid being seen. There were only two other doors on this floor.

"Where are you trying to go?" The woman's voice lost the panicked edge and adopted a flirtatious tone instead.

Fergus laid on the charm. "Right here seems like a nice place to be." I took off running down the hall.

He'll be alone, I reminded myself. *Just go in. Say the words. Get it done. Get out.* I clasped the pendant against my chest as I turned the first doorknob. The door creaked open into a broom closet.

I took a steadying breath as I raced across the hall to the second door. *It's going to be okay. He can't hurt me…* I opened the door quietly and reached behind me to get the 9mm from my back.

The room was dimly lit. The sun beat against the shuttered blinds and a row of black boxes with glowing screens illuminated the center tables.

Where are you, you bastard? I flicked off the safety lever on the gun and softly closed the door behind me.

"What do we have here?" I spun to the direction of the voice coming from my left with the pistol held out in front of me. Three men stood from their seats at the circle table, all pointing their own guns back at me. Kingston sat in his chair with his cruel face twisting into a boorish smile.

"Did my girl come to see me?" he laughed.

Shit. I backed toward the door while Kingston waved his finger like a pendulum.

"Not today," he grinned. "You don't get to run." The mafia thugs rushed forward.

*

I'll always kick myself for hesitating to shoot, it could have saved me the ass kicking that followed. No seriously, one of the thugs kicked me in the ass right after the first one hit me in the head with his pistol and wrestled the gun from my hands as I fell to the ground.

"Check the hall," Kingston ordered.

"There's no one there, boss," the ass kicker called back from the open doorway.

"You're alone again," Kingston grunted as he squatted next to me. "This must be my lucky day."

I placed my hands against the floor and tried to push myself up as I glared at him.

"Still have some fight left I see, Miss Vita," he spit as he drew out my name. "I bet I can take that out of you."

He stood and placed the heel of his shoe against the top of my head, slamming me back down. I tried to scramble away on the floor, but the ass kicker laughed as he grabbed my leg and dragged me to the center of the room.

185

"What do we do with her boss?" one of the other thugs asked.

"I know she had something to do with the system disruption," Kingston smirked. "Why else would she be here? I think we need to get some answers. No reason why we can't have fun getting them."

I climbed to my knees and drew in a ragged breath. "If the government finds out you hurt me, there will be hell to pay."

"For an orphan rat like you?" Kingston chucked. "I bet they don't even know you're here."

Panic gripped me. I knew he was right and the smile that lit up his bulging eyes told me he knew it too. He back handed me across my face, splitting my lip open with one of his rings.

I screamed at the top of my lungs hoping Fergus, or anyone, would hear. The third thug clapped his hand over my mouth as I struggled to get away.

"Stop fighting," he said as he held me pinned against his chest. "This will be easier if you give in."

I managed to get a piece of his finger between my teeth and bit down as hard as I could.

"Stupid bitch." He slammed me onto the floor again.

"She'll never stop fighting," Kingston smiled as he rolled up his sleeves. "That's why I've always been drawn to her. I want to see if I can take the fight away."

*

They made it a game. Dragging me back to the center every time I crawled away, punching me every time I refused to answer. I got punched a lot. Thankfully, I can take a hit. After what felt like an eternity, but in reality would have only been minutes, the thugs stood panting heavily as I curled up on the floor.

"How much longer are we going to do this boss?" one of the thugs asked.

I laid in a state of pure shock and pain, letting the waves crash over me. My only coherent thought was to get up again. I tried to say the words out loud, but my voice was cracked and hoarse from screaming. *I failed.*

"No, you didn't," Vorie's words came clearly into my ears.

"Yes I did," I whispered.

"You're the strongest person I know, and you're not done yet."

"It hurts," I coughed.

"No shit. Get up."

"I don't know how to get out of this. They have my gun."

"Use what you have. Where is the pendant?"

"That stupid thing was supposed to give me strength and it's not working," I mumbled.

"Who is she talking to?" The thugs walked back over to me. Suddenly, the blinds began to shake as if some ghostly spirit was haunting the building. The men froze as they stared at the window and I smiled as I spit out a mouthful of blood.

I reached inside my shirt and pulled out the pendant. Then I jammed the spike of the star into the back of ass kicker's knee. He fell to the floor screaming and I ripped his pistol from the holster. Just as I fired at the thug who'd taken my gun, the door burst open and Fergus came rushing in.

He didn't hesitate to shoot.

"Not him." I pointed to Kingston as I shakily rose to my feet. Anger burned through Fergus' eyes as he ran to my side.

"Are you okay?" he asked, never taking his eyes off Kingston.

"I'm fine." I ran my tongue over my teeth, trying to soothe the swelling of my lips. "What took you so long?"

"I'll explain later," he shook his head.

I looked at the dead mafia thugs at our feet. *You're welcome,* I thought.

"You work for us, boy." Kingston glared at Fergus.

"Not anymore," he said coldly. "What do you need him to do?"

"Just get him in the chair. He needs to log into the system." I rubbed my aching head gently with my palm. There were more lumps than I could count.

"I'm not helping you," Kingston laughed.

"You will whether you want to or not," I sighed. Fergus shoved him roughly into a seat in front of a computer.

I pulled the pendant from the dead man's leg and held the chain in my hand. The ancient words came pouring from my bloodied mouth like a song in a voice that wasn't my own.

Virus venire, nunc ire virum

Animis hominum

Similiter etiam non est ita

Ite, nunc prius ad finem

Kingston paled as his fingers began to tap the letter keys in front of him.

Pestem dolorem

Pestem dolor

189

Cras autem tu occidit

Pugnabit torquem naturalis

Malum ultra non amplius dare

Virus fieri, nunc virus relinquo

Res regit vivat et nos

Hoc dixi. Sic fiat semper

"What am I doing?" he cried.

"Nothing." I leaned on Fergus as the screen went blank. "It's already done."

"We shouldn't leave him alive," Fergus said as he wrapped his arm around my waist to help steady me. "He'll tell them it was us."

"He won't remember." I placed the pendant in my pocket. Kingston closed his eyes and a trail of drool spilled down his chin. "I took away his livelihood and his reputation. They'll blame him for what was done. That's a fate much worse than death."

I nodded to the empty office near the stairwell as we passed.

"I had to convince her to meet me for lunch downstairs," he grinned guiltily. "She's probably still waiting."

We made it down the stairs, even though each step was more painful than the last.

"One minute to spare." Juniper pointed angrily at the clock on the dashboard as I sank into the passenger seat. "How did this happen to you?"

"I'm still a shitty shot." I looked at her through my swelling eyelids and shrugged. Then I handed her back the gun before laying my head against the cool glass of the window.

Chapter 16

∞

We left the city as quietly as we entered it. The only difference was the groups of disorientated people we passed on the street corners near the portals. I was suddenly worried about how they were all going to eat, but I closed my eyes and sleep instantly took me away. *One step at a time...*

A few hours later, we stopped at an abandoned town at the base of a purple mountain range that was covered in ancient pine trees. The wind blew cold and dry around us, kicking up dirt over the broken pavement, and swirling it in little tornadoes that danced into the desert.

"Can you see if that truck works?" I pointed across the asphalt parking lot as I leaned against the hood of the Jeep. Fergus nodded and went to inspect it.

"Is this where we part ways?" Juniper asked. Brayson was staring off into the distance, studying the mountain face.

"I think so," I said weakly. "Thank you. For everything."

"I'm proud of you." She shook my hand and then walked away without saying anything further.

"Are you going to be okay?" Brayson asked once we were alone.

"Yeah." I reached over to hug him with one arm. My chest hurt too much to touch. Honestly, lifting my arm hurt too. "Are you?"

"Do I have another choice?"

"No," I giggled as I patted him on the back. "Vorie won't allow it. And Brayson, Astrid is a nice girl. I mean, she's no Vorie, but she's okay."

He smirked as he shook his head. "Take care of yourself and come back to see me some time," he said as he opened the door to the Jeep.

"Are you ready?" Fergus called from the truck.

*

I wish I could say I saw more of the country during the trip, but my throbbing head and all the aches liked it better when I closed my eyes. I did get us a rabbit to eat for dinner on our fifth day of traveling. I was pretty proud of myself for that.

Fergus took the brunt of the driving shifts. I owed him big time. We didn't talk much during the week it took to drive from coast to coast, but I'm sure we were thinking the same thing. *For better or worse, we'd just changed the world. What happens now?*

*

The snow was heavily banked on the sides of the road as we entered D.C. on our eighth day of driving.

"Are you sure you don't want to go to Florida?" Fergus shivered as he turned on the heater.

"Maybe someday," I smiled.

We climbed the steps to the government building. I could move without cringing now, but my face was an ugly shade of swollen purple and yellow.

Alister came walking out of the giant wooden doors as we reached the top step.

"Christ, Fawn!" He dropped his briefcase in the snow. "What happened to you?"

Alister cupped the sides of my face tenderly in his hands as he inspected the thugs' handywork.

"Ran into a wall," I shrugged. His worry snapped to outrage as he turned his glare toward Fergus. I stepped protectively between the two of them.

"If it wasn't for him, I wouldn't be here." I stood toe to toe with Alister, challengingly staring him down. "He saved my life."

"Come on little deer," he sighed in defeat. "I'm just heading to the professor's house. They'll be anxious to see you." He turned toward Fergus, giving him a dismissive glance. "Thank you for helping her and for bringing her back to me. Do you need a vehicle to get where you are going?

"Actually," I smiled brightly, reopening the split on my lip, then groaned as I held my hand against it. "Fergus is staying with me for a while. He's my friend and rumor has it, he makes a great bodyguard. A girl can't be too careful these days. That won't be a problem, right?"

I didn't wait for an answer as I turned and headed down the steps to Alister's waiting car.

"Hurry up," I called back over my shoulder. "I don't want to be late for dinner."

*

Mary had a little lamb...

I sat on the velvet chair in front of the fireplace and laid my book on the stand as Vorie manifested in front of me. The crackle of the burning wood mixed with the sound of her haunting melody in the stillness of the room.

"You still look awful," she smiled.

"Well at least I'm not dead," I smirked.

"Touché."

I moved my legs over so that she had room to sit. It was funny how I continued to make the same movements as if she were really there in flesh and blood, and she continued to act the same too. Old habits die hard, I guess.

"How's Brayson?" I asked her softly, even though I wasn't sure if I wanted to know.

"He's actually on a date right now." Vorie smiled sweetly and folded her hands in her lap.

"Yeah. I didn't want to know that. How are you? Are you okay?"

"Of course." She glanced down at the book I was reading and stared at it silently. "I mean, a small part of me hopes it goes completely awful and she chokes on a chicken bone. But other than that, I'm completely okay."

"Right?" I exclaimed pulling my feet beneath me and excitedly jumping to my knees. "Let's do something to sabotage it! Can you do the haunted house thing like you did at the portal system office?"

"No," she laughed. "I'm not going to do anything. I want them to have a nice time."

"You're a better person than I am." I shook my head.

"Eh," Vorie winked. "You're alright too. I mean, you did single handedly take down the whole portal system."

"It was not single handedly at all. If you and Fergus weren't there, and if Medea hadn't given me the tools, I wouldn't have been able to do anything."

"Stop being so modest." She rolled her ghostly eyes. "Speaking of Fergus, how's that all working out?"

"He's actually down the hall if you want to go talk to him." I laughed as she gave me a blank stare. "He's not so bad. The professor kind of likes him. They've been discussing the clinics that the mafia sends destroyers to. Turns out they just use those clinics as schools to train them to work. And Freida loves him. He reminds her of Odan I think. Except Odan doesn't like him. Serves the kid right."

"And what about Alister? What does he think?"

"Oh, you know. He is fine with it," I lied.

"This isn't going to turn into some cliché love triangle type thing, is it?" She raised an eyebrow.

"Ew, no." I shuddered. "Alister is my soul mate and Fergus is just a friend. Plus, I like having him around. He intimidates Reynolds." I gave her a devious grin.

"I guess we will see how this plays out in the future," she smiled back at me.

"No," I groaned as I put my head in my hands. "I don't ever want to hear the word future ever again. I'm done with all that. I did my job. Destiny can leave me alone now."

"What? Do you think you're just going to stop living and do nothing?" Vorie giggled. "Everyone has a future. You don't get to stop that, even if yours seems like a messed up one."

I peeked through my fingers. "How messed up are we talking here? What else could possibly happen?"

Vorie smiled her beautiful smile, exposing her pearly teeth. Her eyes sparked with mischief as she leaned back against the chair. "Oh come on, you know I can't tell you that."

*

Before you go…

Did you like this story? Did you hate it? I really want
to hear what you think. Please consider leaving a
review. Indie authors can't survive without word of
mouth referrals and reviews from readers like you.

Thanks for reading!

Follow the author on Facebook

www.facebook.com/heathercarsonauthor

Instagram

www.instagram.com/heathercarsonauthor

TikTok @heathercarsonauthor

Make sure to sign up for the mailing list to get your
free short story "Katrina's Story" a prelude to the
Project Dandelion series

www.heatherkcarson.com

Other works by Heather Carson

*Sent to a fallout shelter to survive a nuclear catastrophe, a
group of teenagers are the last hope for humanity. Can they
survive living with one another first?*

Get the *Project Dandelion* series, now in one convenient
box set

https://www.amazon.com/Project-Dandelion-
Books-Heather-Carson-ebook/dp/B088J6Z9Q7/

Or see that the readers are saying about this YA post-apocalyptic series, book 1-

https://www.amazon.com/Project-Dandelion-Heather-Carson-ebook/dp/B07TLF8HN7/

Printed in Great Britain
by Amazon